Noah felt a chill work across him. He suddenly realized how cold and quiet the tunnel was.

Tank said, "He went that way, that's for sure."

From the nearby curtain, something suddenly swung out—an arm with a mangy mess of hair. Curled claws sliced through the air, and a muscular hand seized Tank's arm. The big man was pulled off his feet and yanked through the portal.

THE SECRET ZOO

RIDDLES AND DANGER

BRYAN CHICK

GREENWILLOW BOOKS
An Imprint of HarperCollinsPublishers

The Secret Zoo: Riddles and Danger
Copyright © 2011 by Bryan Chick

The text of this book is set in Arrus BT
Book design by Paul Zakris

Library of Congress Cataloging-in-Publication Data

Chick, Bryan.
Riddles and danger / by Bryan Chick.
p. cm. — (The secret zoo)
"Greenwillow Books."
Summary: Having discovered a magical society beneath the exhibits at the Clarksville City Zoo where animals and humans live harmoniously together as equals, Noah and his friends must protect the secret zoo at all costs.
ISBN 978-0-06-198927-8 (trade bdg.)
ISBN 978-0-06-198928-5 (pbk.)
[1. Zoos—Fiction. 2. Zoo animals—Fiction. 3. Secret societies—Fiction. 4. Human-animal relationships—Fiction. 5. Magic—Fiction. 6. Friendship—Fiction.] I. Title.
PZ7.C4336Ri 2011   [Fic]—dc22   2011005930

12 13 14 15 16 LP/BR 10 9 8 7 6 5 4 3 2 1
First Edition

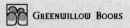 GREENWILLOW BOOKS

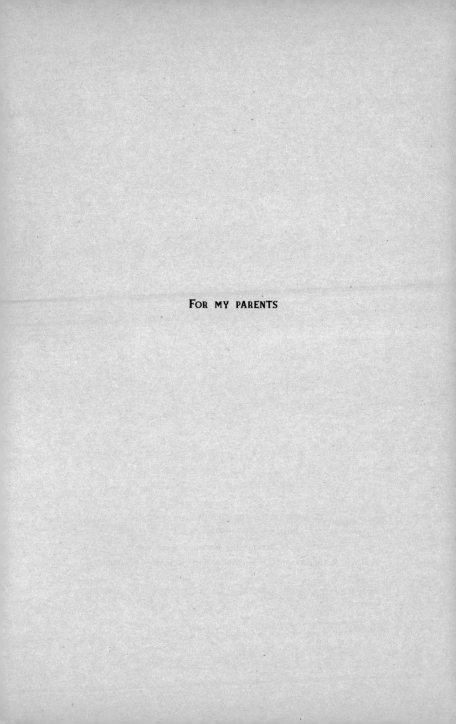

FOR MY PARENTS

Tracks in the Grottoes

As Tank walked across the Clarksville Zoo, all was quiet and dark. A few stars speckled the otherwise black sky, and light fell in the shape of cones from scattered lampposts. The cold December wind had worked the warmth from his body. At Chinchillavilla, a small stone building draped in ivy, he unlocked the door, then stepped inside, his palms rubbing together.

An open exhibit, Chinchillavilla had a terrain that was dry and rocky, covered with holes and crevices. Boulders lay around, and the prickly stems of cacti punched skyward. The façades of old country homes were built into the walls, creating the impression of a villa. The houses had white walls, arched doorways, and colorful roof tiles made of clay. Brick sidewalks ran through patches of tall grass, connecting front doors. Dozens of chinchillas lay around, most of them sleeping.

Tank strolled off the visitor path and took a seat in a wooden rocking chair on the porch of a house. He breathed warm air across his hands, cocked his head back, and began to rock. Beneath his massive weight, the chair creaked and groaned. He closed his eyes. A minute passed, then another. His breathing slowed, and his thoughts dimmed. Without meaning to, he dozed off.

He awoke sometime later when he felt something tugging on the laces of his boots. He sat up with a jolt to see the porch covered with chinchillas, as many as a hundred. They'd come from a doorway in the wall that contained a hidden passage to the Secret Zoo, and now they were trying to climb his legs, the puny pads of their feet stroking his pants, their whiskers and oversized ears twitching. Their tiny grunts and barks filled the air. Something was wrong.

The big man jumped to his feet, sending the chair into a wild rock that scattered dozens of chinchillas.

"Easy, easy," Tank said. "What's wrong?"

The animals turned all at once and flooded back through the door. Tank followed, careful not to flatten any beneath his size twenty-two boots. Once the last of the chinchillas had skittered past him, he eased the door shut, triggering on a few lights. Directly in front of him was a corridor leading into the ground. Lined with dusty bricks, it was barely large enough to fit him. He had entered the Grottoes, a magical staging area into the Secret Zoo and distant parts of the Clarksville Zoo.

The chinchillas led him down a steep ramp to where the tunnel leveled out. The Grottoes continued straight for at least fifty feet. On both sides of the passage were branches to new tunnels with dusty velvet curtains draped over their mouths. Above each opening was a thin metal plate engraved with words. One read "Metr-APE-olis." Another read "The Secret Chinchillavilla." Another read "A-Lotta-Hippopotami." There were eight tunnel branches in all.

The chinchillas began to bark at a place on the ground. Tank dropped his gaze and saw the unmistakable prints of a sasquatch in the dirt. Snowy and wet, they started at a tunnel marked "The Secret Arctic Town." A chill ran through him. Though the sasquatches were loose in the Secret Zoo, they'd never crossed its magical threshold to reach as far as the Grottoes.

The big man ran forward, his broad shoulders nearly sweeping the walls, chinchillas dodging out of his path. He traced the tracks to where they disappeared through a branch marked "The Knickknack and Snack Shack." He followed the markings up a steep flight of stairs and pushed through an overhead hatch door, emerging inside a Clarksville Zoo gift shop. Muddy footprints revealed how the sasquatch had roamed around before turning back to the Grottoes.

Chinchillas flooded into the gift shop, filling it with the soft patter of their steps. They scampered in all directions, sniffing the ground and trampling across the footprints.

The front wall of the Knickknack and Snack Shack was mostly glass. Tank stared out into a view along the eastern side of the zoo. He saw several outdoor exhibits and, beyond them, the tall concrete wall that divided the property from the surrounding neighborhood. There the trees were sparse, and in one of them Tank spotted Fort Scout, the elaborate tree fort that Noah and his friends played in.

"What were you doing out here?" Tank asked, as if he were talking to the sasquatch. "Why didn't you—"

He stopped short as the answer struck him. Without another thought, he turned and rushed down the steps, chinchillas scattering at his feet. He ran though the Grottoes toward the Secret Zoo. He needed to get to Mr. Darby, the leader of the magical kingdom, and let him know what he'd just discovered.

A sasquatch had been scouting the Clarksville Zoo, looking for the best way to invade Noah's neighborhood.

❦ CHAPTER 1 ❧

KANGAROO KAMPGROUND

"Richie!" Ella called out. "C'mon already!"

Richie, who was bent down on one knee, finished tightening the laces on his running shoes—the kind he was noted for, a flashy pair with swirls of vibrant color—and hurried after his friends, the Action Scouts, who'd just stepped through the front entrance of the Clarksville Zoo. At the gates, Richie pitched his hip forward, plowed through a turnstile, and quickly caught up to Ella, Noah, and Megan.

It being only nine-fifteen on a cold Saturday morning, the zoo was all but empty. The air was heavy and humid.

An overnight dusting of snow was beginning to melt, its wetness pasting dead leaves to their shoes.

The four friends were dressed for the weather. Ella wore her usual earmuffs, fluffy pink things that resembled globs of cotton candy. Megan wore her sporty outdoor headband, which allowed her thick pigtails to droop down. Richie wore his stocking cap, his head circled by a bulky ribbed cuff and crowned with a bushy pom-pom. And Noah wore his now-favorite hunting cap, which Blizzard and Podgy, two animals from the Secret Zoo, had given him. Bright red with big earflaps, it was every bit as goofy as Richie's hat, but it was warm, and Noah liked how it reminded him of his first journey into the magical world just beyond his backyard.

The zoo was decked out for its annual Festival of Lights. Countless colorful bulbs dangled from eaves and coiled around fence rails. Even the trees in some outdoor exhibits were decorated.

"Remind me where crosstraining is today," Ella said. Her ponytail jumped across her shoulders as she scanned her friends.

"Kangaroo Kampground," answered Megan.

It had been only a week since their last full-scale adventure with the Secret Zoo. The scouts had spent this time training as Crossers, Secret Cityzens who traveled between the ordinary zoo and its magical counterpart.

Mr. Darby had assigned a number of Secret Cityzens to assist in their training: a hulking man named Tank; four teenagers known as the Descenders; and a group of animals that included Blizzard, a powerful polar bear; Podgy, a flying penguin; P-Dog, a rambunctious prairie dog; Little Bighorn, a bold rhinoceros; and Marlo, a king-fisher that served as a messenger bird, delivering notes between Mr. Darby and the scouts.

In classroomlike settings held in various exhibits, the scouts had begun to study the wondrous world of the Secret Zoo. They'd discussed the history of the Secret Society, a band of humans and animals living in har-mony, and learned why it existed—primarily to protect every animal species from extinction. They'd learned about the Secret Council and its principles for govern-ing. They'd learned about the magic that had helped create the Secret Zoo—how it had flowed from Kavita, the world's only real magician, to eventually power her four sons, each born to a different mother thousands of years later. They'd learned about "straight drops," tun-nels that led directly from the Clarksville Zoo to areas in the Secret Zoo known as sectors. These sectors resem-bled the zoo exhibits joined to them, only on a grander scale, and they connected to the core of the Secret Zoo, the City of Species, which was crowded with animals and people and built in a lush forest.

The scouts crosstrained at least twice a week. Their parents believed they were serving as zoo volunteers as part of a program hosted by their school. Living next to the Clarksville Zoo made this easy. The four friends could walk out their front doors, meet at the zoo, train, and be home in less than two hours. On school days it was even easier. The children could swing by the zoo on their walk home, spend some time crosstraining, and still beat dinner to their tables. As incredible as it seemed, it was simple for the four of them to maintain their normal lives while being members of a secret civilization. They could be studying math one hour, then riding a polar bear the next.

Now, they neared Kangaroo Kampground. The exhibit was in a new log building that deliberately looked old. Flat logs were stacked high, their corners interlocked. A gable roof sat on rafters that protruded beyond the outside walls. A wide boulder chimney helped frame one side of the structure. The front booth of the exhibit seemed a dilapidated shack at the world's most rustic campsite. A weathered wooden sign read "Kangaroo Kampground! Jump on in!"

Richie glanced at his watch. "Nine-thirty. Right on time."

The front steps squealed and moaned as the scouts headed up them. The foursome stopped at the front doors, where a metal sign spoiled the rustic ambience. Across its silvery sheen, bold black letters read "CLOSED FOR CONSTRUCTION!" Knowing this really meant "CLOSED FOR CROSSTRAINING!" Noah dug into his pocket for the magic key that could open any door at the Clarksville Zoo and seated it into the slot. With a *click!* the door popped open. The scouts glanced over their shoulders to make certain no one was looking and slipped inside.

The exhibit was an open type where visitors could walk freely among the animals—dozens of kangaroos in this case. Trees and plants grew in the large space, and light poured in from a few big windows. Several zoo employees normally patrolled the open exhibit, but now it was empty.

The scouts stepped onto the main visitor aisle, a dirt path pitted with small holes. Campsite items were all around—tents, picnic tables, barbecue grills, and fire pits with piles of fake logs that seemed to smolder. Occasional signs pretended to show the direction of campsite attractions with painted arrows: "Pool Area," "Playground," "Showers," "Vending." Blinking Christmas lights dangled from the heights.

Kangaroos were scattered about. Most were lounging on their sides, looking bored. A few, seeing the scouts, jumped to attention. With their powerful hind legs, rabbitlike ears, doelike eyes, and jumbo feet, they seemed like caricatures put together from the features of other animals. Several hopped over to the path and curiously sniffed the four friends.

"Hey, dudes," Ella said as she reached out her hand, donned in a pink winter glove, and playfully tapped their heads. One kangaroo lapped its long tongue against her sleeve.

The scouts turned down a path that led to the entrance of a big tent. Inside was a series of ten aluminum benches, equally spaced. Toward the front of the tent, a television was mounted high on a pole. Normally this television looped a ten-minute video detailing kangaroo habits, but today it was turned off. Between the pole and the first row of benches stood a portable whiteboard. Beside it was a teenager with a knit cap pulled over his eyebrows and a scraggly beard dangling from his chin. It was Tameron, one of the Descenders assigned to crosstrain the scouts. He peered out from under the short brim of his cap. "What's up?"

Noah nodded as the scouts took seats along a bench toward the middle.

Tameron planted his foot on the bench in front of him. He looked like an army sergeant ready to grill a squad of soldiers who'd messed up in a serious way.

"A couple days ago," Tameron began, "we had an incident."

"Uh-oh," Ella said. "An *incident*. Already this doesn't sound good."

"Tank was in the Grottoes and guess what he found? Sasquatch tracks."

The scouts winced. They all knew the sasquatches had never reached as far as the Grottoes.

Tameron continued. "He tracked the prints into a gift shop along the east wall of the zoo."

"The Knickknack and Snack Shack," Megan said. "That's right by Fort Scout. You can see it from our tree."

Tameron nodded.

"Did it get out?" Megan asked.

"Didn't look like it. The tracks went straight back to the Grottoes. Tank thinks it was scouting the area, looking for the easiest way to invade your neighborhood."

Fear moved Noah's insides.

"This is *sooooo* not good," Richie said.

"The east wall . . ." Noah said. "That's the part you guys have trouble guarding at night. Because there aren't many trees, you can't post animals along it, right?"

Tameron nodded. "If the sasquatches decide to move on that part of the wall, we might not spot them until it's too late."

Ella said, "So not only do we have to stop the Shadowist from getting *in* the zoo, now we have to stop the sasquatches from getting *out*!" Everyone knew the Shadowist as the near-mythical man trying to get inside the Secret Zoo.

"Things just got more complicated," Tameron said. He seemed to consider something, then added, "What do you guys know about the patrols, the ones we do at night?"

"Only what you've taught us," Ella said, "which is"—she stared into the corners of her eyes and scanned her thoughts—"pretty much nothing."

"Well, that's about to change right now."

Richie greedily rubbed his hands together. "Sweetness! The perimeter patrols! I've been waiting to hear about this for weeks! Spare no detail!"

"I'll recap what we know," Megan volunteered. "There's the concrete wall, obviously. It goes all around the zoo. It's about fifteen feet high and surrounded by huge trees. You guys guard the zoo at night by somehow getting animals into those trees. The animals look out for DeGraff, the Shadowist."

"This part has always baffled me," Noah said. "I mean, the animals . . . what kind can possibly sneak into our trees?"

Ella said, "Probably not elephants, I'm thinking."

"Mostly small, arboreal animals," Tameron said.

"Ar-bo-*what*-e-al?" Ella said. She passed a curious stare across the group of Crossers and said, "Did we just switch languages or something?"

Richie jumped at the opportunity to demonstrate his knowledge. "Arboreal animals—they dwell in trees."

Tameron nodded. "Along the perimeter wall we post koalas, lemurs, galagos, and all kinds of possums. A few others, too. Almost all of them are nocturnal—we need them because they see good in the dark. We also use owls and bats. And prairie dogs, but they have a different role."

Noah felt his jaw drop. "All these animals . . . right there in our backyard trees. How do they *not* get spotted?"

"Oh, they've been spotted," Tameron said. "Quite a few times."

"Huh?"

"Remember about seven years ago when two lemurs were spotted on Zinnia Street in a tree in some lady's backyard?"

The scouts nodded. Though they were too young to recall the incident, they'd heard the story.

"That was us. The lemurs were on watch. The lady called the police, who dispatched Animal Control. They trapped the lemurs and shipped them back to the zoo."

"Any others?" Richie asked.

"A few," Tameron replied. "People sometimes see our owls, but they don't think nothing about that. And our prairie dogs—they're always getting spotted. But people think they're squirrels. Or gophers."

"Unreal," Megan said, shaking her head.

"There's more," Tameron said.

"There usually is with you guys," said Ella.

"The animals don't stop at the trees around the zoo wall—they go into the trees throughout your whole neighborhood."

"You've got to be kidding me," Megan said.

"We only use tarsiers for this."

"Tarsiers?" Noah said. "What are they?"

"You're going to find out in just a little bit."

Ella said, "Well, whatever they are—how in the world do they make it down our streets without getting noticed?"

"Tunnels," Tameron answered.

"In our neighborhood?" Richie said.

"Yep. They branch off the Grottoes and go everywhere. They're built and maintained by our prairie dogs. They work in them every night—cleaning out debris, widening them, extending them, burrowing new ones, and closing off old ones that are no longer needed."

"Way, way, way cool," said Richie. "This is the kind of cool you only see in the movies."

"Why don't people notice holes in their yards?" Ella asked. "I mean, the tarsiers have to come out somewhere."

"You tell me," Tameron said. "It's your neighborhood. You ever see weird holes in your grass?"

The scouts shook their heads.

"The prairie dogs aren't dumb. Their tunnels rise up

in private spots. Beneath bushes, sheds, decks. Into the open space beneath porches. Inside dark tree hollows. All kinds of places."

"How many tunnels?" Richie asked. "If you had to guess."

Tameron shrugged. "Don't know. It's a big neighborhood, kid. Hundreds, I guess."

"Hundreds!" Richie gasped.

"Like I said . . . I don't really know. Teach P-Dog to talk and maybe he'll tell you."

Just then a kangaroo hopped into the tent and stopped at the back bench. He looked different from the others because one of his ears was bent sideways, as if broken. The way his short front arms dangled in front of his stomach reminded Noah of a T. rex. He poked his snout toward the scouts and sniffed the scents out of the air, seeming a bit surprised at the gathering, his eyes wide and unblinking.

Noah said, "For all the time the tarsiers spend outside the zoo—eight, nine hours a night—they never get noticed. That's amazing."

"Your neighborhood's dark. No streetlights. And the trees are big and full. Even in the winter you can't see anything in them—all the branches blend together. And the tarsiers, they're practically . . ." Tameron's voice trailed off. "Well, you're about to see."

Megan said, "Do animals patrol from inside the zoo at night?"

"Yeah. Mostly in the trees and places with a good view of the grounds—the taller exhibits. We put them where there's almost zero risk of being seen."

"Any other animals?" Richie asked.

Tameron nodded. "Owls. And bats—lots of bats. We use them for their echolocation."

"What?" Ella said. "Echolocomotion? Isn't that a song at a wedding reception—the one where everyone stumbles around in a line, pretending to be a train?"

"Echolocation," Richie said, anxious as ever to share his trivia knowledge. "It's a way to tell where something is by the echo it makes. Bats use it to help them see at night—to locate prey."

"Yep," Tameron said. "And guess what the prey is in this case."

"DeGraff," Noah said. "The Shadowist. But how can the bats tell him apart from anyone else?"

"Remember what we told you about DeGraff? That he's part human and part shadow, his decaying body kept together by the magic in the shadows?"

"It's kind of hard to forget a thing like that," Ella said. "It's the kind of thing that hangs out in your brain, giving you nightmares and stuff."

"His body gives off a very distinct sound. Our bats . . . they've been trained to pick it up."

Noah thought about this. It made sense. Objects produced different echoes. Surely DeGraff's body would give off a sound like no other.

"Okay," Richie said. "Besides the tarsiers and the other arboreal animals, we have owls and bats. . . . and prairie dogs digging tunnels. Anything else?"

"Monkeys," Tameron said. "Police-monkeys. We usually have around ten circling the zoo. They move in groups of two or three."

Richie said, "Always on our rooftops, right?"

"Yeah," Tameron answered. "And the trees. They try to keep off the ground."

"How is it possible that we don't hear them?" Ella asked.

"We use smaller monkeys—night monkeys, spider monkeys, and others that see well at night. They don't weigh much. And they move so swiftly that they hardly make a sound."

The kangaroo that had entered the tent hopped up to the scouts and stopped beside Ella, who was sitting closest to the aisle.

"What's up, bub?" Ella asked.

The kangaroo tipped his head to one side and then the other, studying Ella. The end of his bent ear dangled limply.

"What's his name?"

"Punchy," Tameron answered. "He likes to punch things."

Ella scrunched up her face at the kangaroo and said, "Don't even think about it—not unless you're looking for a black eye."

Tameron steered the conversation back, saying, "The monkeys stay on the backs of the roofs—the sides that face the zoo. You can't see them from the street. And the monkeys are smart. If they see someone, they avoid all the nearby houses and move quietly through the trees. They've only been spotted once, and that was by some girl in a tree fort." Tameron raised an eyebrow at Megan, who offered a weak smile in a half-apologetic way. "Can you guys think of anything else that you know about the perimeter patrols?"

Silence was the scouts' response.

"Let me see if I can fill in the blanks. There are three main groups of Secret Cityzens involved: owls, other animals, and Descenders—me, Hannah, Sam, and Solana." He turned to the whiteboard and drew a large square. "Okay—here's the Clarksville Zoo."

"Looks just like it," Ella teased as she tipped her head to one side, pretending to contemplate the drawing as one might fine art. "Just like the view from a satellite, only better."

Tameron circled the top line of the square and wrote the letter *S*. He then circled the other sides of the square and marked the circles *E*, *N*, and *W*. "The territories," he said.

"Practically like using my mom's GPS," Ella quipped.

Tameron scowled at Ella. "You going to be making jokes the whole time?"

Ella shifted her eyes nervously. "Ummm . . . I'm thinking that was probably the last one for a while."

"Good." Tameron turned back to the drawing and said, "Four territories. Thirty, maybe forty owls assigned to each one. Each territory has a single type of owl dedicated to it. We use the smallest ones we got—pygmy owls and elf owls, which are the smallest in the world, barely the size of a sparrow. The owls perch in the highest spots in the trees, places that have good views of the neighborhood. We let them out around ten. At the same time we release the bats. The bats aren't assigned to a specific territory; instead, they continuously circle the zoo. Got it so far?"

The scouts nodded.

"Around ten-thirty, we release the animals. The ones that post in the trees along the wall just jump into them. The tarsiers move into your neighborhood through the prairie dog tunnels. Once they're out, they climb the trees and quickly settle into their posts."

The scouts stopped their questions and absorbed this new information. Noah realized the wonder and mystery of the Secret Zoo never seemed to end—seemed, in fact, to always be evolving into something greater, something more magnificent.

"Okay," Ella said. "So we've now got owls and a bunch of *ar-bo-what-ev-er-eal* things in our trees. What about you and your buds?"

Tameron said, "We post around the zoo. We stick to tall structures, something with a view. The water tower, Metr-APE-olis—places like that."

Richie said, "But the animals . . . what do they do if they spot DeGraff?"

"They're trained to report the sighting back to the nearest Descender."

"How?" asked Ella.

"The owls. Their purpose is to keep watch on the animals in the trees. If an arboreal animal spots DeGraff, it'll shake a branch to alert the owls. An owl will swoop in, confirm the sighting, then fly to the nearest Descender, who knows to treat the owl's arrival as a message that DeGraff's been seen. The Descender will contact the guards at the Clarksville Zoo using one of these." Tameron touched his ear, where a tiny earset with no visible wires was mounted. "They're just sophisticated radios," he explained. "The guards wear them, too. Once the guards get the message, a few will team up with the Descender and follow the owl to the place DeGraff was spotted."

Megan asked, "But that'll take some time—what if DeGraff goes somewhere else?"

"The animals are trained to show his location by shaking branches." Tameron paused, then explained it another way: "They follow him from the treetops."

The scouts contemplated everything they'd just heard. Ideas and thoughts roamed in Noah's head, creating images. His gaze wandered. On the ground was Tameron's canvas backpack. The size of an army pack, it had bulging pockets with zippers and buckles and snaps. Velvet patches were stitched to it. Though they seemed to be decorative, Noah understood their real purpose. They supplied the magic that enabled the thing inside the canvas bag to join to Tameron, becoming a natural extension of his body—an extremity that he could control. Coiled inside the backpack was Tameron's tail, his special power as a Descender.

Noah turned to Ella and saw Punchy poke his snout forward and sniff one of her poofy earmuffs. The kangaroo softly punched it, then curiously looked her over.

"Kanga dude," Ella said, "they're not my real ears, you know." To demonstrate, she pulled out one earmuff and let it snap back into place. Punchy jumped away a few feet, startled and suspicious of Ella's large, pink, retractable ear. He hopped behind the scouts to where Richie sat and took an interest in him.

Richie, looking nervous, scooted down the bench. "What do you want?"

Punchy plunged his snout into the softball-sized pom-pom on his cap, sniffed, then sneezed all over Richie.

"Ewww," Ella said to Richie. "Kanga boogers. That's really, really gross."

The kangaroo reached up his thumbless forelimb and angrily punched the pom-pom, the thing that had made him sneeze.

Richie grabbed his hat by the cuff and held it down. "Hey! Go pick on Ella's earmuffs again!"

Noah, Ella, and Megan broke into a laugh. After a bit, Tameron turned back to his rudimentary drawing of the Clarksville Zoo. He drew a small square in four spots along the inside of the zoo, each one near a different wall. "Lookout points for the Descenders. One Descender per lookout point. We rotate to stay fresh." He then shaded in areas along the zoo border, saying, "Trees." Then, on the outside of the wooden area, he drew little triangles. "The houses that back to the trees."

"It's like Google Earth," Ella said. "Look! I think I see my mailbox!"

Tameron touched the circles representing the territories, saying, "Remember, one type of owl is assigned to each territory." He swapped his black marker for a red one, then dropped dots in each of the circles. "Their only purpose is to watch for alerts from the animals and communicate them back to the Descenders." He traded the red marker for a blue one and drew a cluster of spots. "The bats." Dragging a dashed line around the zoo, he said, "They fly around the zoo all night." He grabbed a green marker and bespeckled a triangular shape that represented a house. "The police-monkeys. They move through the trees and across the rooftops." He picked up a yellow marker and drew a scattered cluster of dots all around the zoo. "The prairie dogs. They're responsible for the tunnels." Then, with a purple marker, he spotted the trees. "The rest of the arboreal animals. Tarsiers, when you get away from the wall." He drew a small square outside the eastern wall and scrawled the letters *F* and *S* inside it. "Fort Scout," he said.

"Ah yes," Ella said. "Our home away from home." She squinted at the picture. "Look, there's Richie playing with his electro-toys!"

Tameron stared out at the scouts from the shadow of his brim. With his scraggly beard and his arms crossed over his chest, he looked just about like the toughest guy Noah had ever seen. He looked, in fact, like someone who might punch you in the head just for the fun of it. He turned back to the whiteboard and studied his elementary drawing, tipping his head from side to side. "There's just one thing we need to change."

"What's that?" Noah asked.

"We need to change this . . ." With the palm of his hand,

Tameron wiped out one of the four squares that represented the Descenders' lookout points. Then he picked up a black marker and drew a similar square around Fort Scout. ". . . to this."

As Noah realized what Tameron was getting at, his whole body clenched.

"What are you trying to say?" Ella asked.

It was Noah who answered. "He wants to move one of the lookout points to Fort Scout to keep a better watch on the east wall."

The other scouts, wide-eyed with disbelief, stared at Tameron.

With a smirk, Tameron said, "You guys got it wrong. That's not what *I'm* saying at all. It's Darby doing the talking." He lifted his backpack, punched his arms through its straps, and headed for the exit of the tent, saying, "C'mon, let's go see the boss."

The scouts hurried out into Kangaroo Kampground and followed the brawny Descender toward a place in the exhibit that would magically deliver them to the Secret Zoo.

CHAPTER 2

The Secret Kangaroo Kampground

"Here," Tameron said. "This is it."

The Crossers were in the rear of Kangaroo Kampground near a tent that was big enough for at least ten adults to stand in. The two flaps of the tent's only door were draped closed. Punchy was standing beside Richie, his puny arms dangling in front of his stomach.

"The gateway," Tameron continued. "To the Secret Kangaroo Kampground. It's on the back wall of this tent. Straight access to the Secret Zoo—no Grottoes."

The Descender led everyone inside. Punchy jumped

forward and squeezed into a spot between Richie and Ella near the middle of the tent.

"Comfy?" Ella asked.

Punchy turned and curiously sniffed her earmuffs again.

The back wall of the tent was made of velvet, the kind that contained the magic necessary to cross into the Secret Zoo. Just beyond it, the scouts knew, was the Secret Kangaroo Kampground.

"Who's first?" Tameron asked.

"Me," said Megan. She stepped forward and pushed against the wall, which gave way on all sides except the top. The curtain draped across her shoulders and then down her back. A second later, she was gone.

Ella went next, and Punchy hopped after her. Richie followed. In the near-empty tent, Tameron swept his arm toward the gateway and invited Noah to have at it. Noah did. As the velvet stroked his body, he felt the familiar tingle of the magic moving into him. The cloth dropped against his heels, and Noah was sent to the Secret Zoo.

The Secret Kangaroo Kampground was like a big and extravagant version of the kangaroo exhibit in the Clarksville Zoo. Covering as much as two square miles, the sector resembled a forested campground. Streaks of sunlight fell from a ceiling of tall, full trees. Countless kangaroos were lounging on their sides or hopping about.

Between hundreds of tents were picnic tables, wooden signs, and fire pits. All the tents had velvet flaps for doors—magical gateways.

At least thirty people were scattered about. They wore green lab coats and carried clipboards with thick stacks of paper. A few walked in and out of the velvet doors. Magical scientists—the scouts had seen them before.

"What are they doing?" Megan asked.

"The scientists?" Tameron asked. When Megan nodded, he said, "They're studying the magic—manipulating it to create new portals."

"Portals?"

Tameron steered a confused look at her. "C'mon—you guys know about portaling."

The scouts shook their heads.

Sounding a bit disgusted, Tameron said, "The gateways that you've been jumping through—they're portals. Just seconds ago, when you passed through that velvet wall of the tent in the Clarksville Zoo, you portaled. To another world, in fact. Portaling . . . it's when something instantly moves across two distant spots. Thanks to Bhanu and his brothers, the magic of portaling is all over the Secret Zoo. Our scientists study it and use this sector to test their findings, portaling from one tent to the next."

Megan said, "But in this case they don't have any real purpose, right?"

"To Crossers they do. We use them to quickly cross the sector, jumping from one tent to the next. The hard part is remembering how the tents connect. It's kind of like a maze without walls."

Noah scanned the far reaches of the sector and saw a light blinking above a tent, marking the gateway into the City of Species, their destination. The area between looked like a crowded suburb of tiny canvas houses. "You have the route memorized?"

"More or less," Tameron said.

A kangaroo jumped up to Noah and became curious about one of the earflaps on his hat. The animal touched it with a stiff forelimb, nervously pulled back its head, then hopped away.

"Okay," Ella said to Tameron. "Lead the way, I guess."

"Just do like I do," Tameron said. "And try to keep up."

The Descender charged forward, straight into the sprawl of tents and kangaroos. He dodged left and right, avoiding the things in his path.

"Hey!" Megan called. "Wait up!"

As the scouts followed him, kangaroos jumped out of the way, their dark eyes wide with fright and their pointy ears twitching toward different sounds.

"*Mooovvve!*" Ella called out to the kangaroos.

Tameron found a tent of interest and disappeared through the portal. As the velvet door swept across Noah, magic surged through his body, and he instantaneously crossed space to exit another tent deeper in the sector. Startled by his sudden appearance, a nearby crowd of kangaroos scattered, their powerful hind legs thrusting against the earth. Noah tripped on a tail and almost stumbled to the ground.

Noah sensed something running beside him and turned to see Punchy. The kangaroo met his gaze in how-you-doing? fashion, then casually looked away.

Tameron quickly led the scouts through another tent entrance, and the Crossers portaled to a new spot. Noah glanced back to see they were already halfway across the Secret Kangaroo Kampground.

As the scouts followed Tameron to a new gateway, a frightened kangaroo darted across their path and crashed into Ella. Right before Noah portaled, he saw his friend lose her balance, then stumble through the velvet curtain of a neighboring tent, unintentionally portaling to a new spot, far away from the group.

CHAPTER 3

ELLA GETS PUNCHY WITH PUNCHY

Ella crashed onto her rear end in a herd of kangaroos that immediately took off in all directions. She stood, adjusted her earmuffs, and scanned the grounds. Tents were everywhere, their velvet flap doors hanging down. The scouts were nowhere in sight, and she couldn't see the flashing light that marked the city gateway. She had no idea where she was in relation to where she'd been.

"Great . . ." she moaned. She cupped her hands to her mouth. *"Megan!"*

No answer. A kangaroo hopped up to her and jabbed its

long snout toward her face. Its nose twitched as it sniffed the air.

"Beat it, Mr. Bounces," Ella said. "I'm in no mood."

The kangaroo swung around and hopped away, looking insulted, its eyes half closed, its ears pulled back.

Ella dusted off her pants and said, "Well, I'll have to do this myself, I guess."

She started jogging, her ponytail swinging behind her. Seconds later, she pushed through the velvet door of a tent and portaled to a new spot, where she crashed into a magical scientist.

"Sorry!" she spat out.

Eyes wide behind beady glasses, the scientist straightened his lab coat and propped his fists on his hips. "You know, you shouldn't be . . . Megan?"

Ella shook her head. "No, the other one."

"Ella?"

"Bingo." Ella was used to being recognized. After finding their way into the Secret Zoo, the scouts were near-celebrities, adored by most, despised by a few.

"Are you crosstraining?" the scientist asked. "Where are—"

"What's the best way to the city gateway? Through the portals, I mean."

The scientist shrugged his shoulders. "I haven't the foggiest idea. The Crossers are the ones always in such a hurry. Me . . . I see no foul in taking my time. I find a casual stroll often clears my head and allows for good—"

"Thanks," Ella cut in as she took off running again.

She weaved around a few tents and then spotted the city gateway. Off to her left, the flashing light was still a great distance away. She chose a new portal at random and dove through, ending up this time on the left of the flashing light, farther away than before.

"You've got to be kidding me," she groaned.

She ran through a new mob of kangaroos, found a magic tent, and portaled again, this time ending up farther than ever. Disgusted, she ran to a new tent, then another, then another, each time portaling to completely random parts of the Secret Kangaroo Kampground, startling the kangaroos into a frenzy.

A few jumps later, she wound up somewhere near the middle of the campground. In the distance she could faintly detect the blinking light. Tameron and the scouts were standing beneath it. Tameron had his arms held out to his sides in a what-the-heck-are-you-doing? way.

"How did you get over there!" Ella hollered.

She sensed someone standing behind her and swung around. Standing there was Punchy. He reached out and thumped Ella's chest.

"Oww!" Ella barked. She cocked a fist and punched the shoulder of his forelimb. "How do you like it, you big lug!"

She heard her name being called and turned back around. Beyond the far-reaching cluster of tents, Noah had his hands cupped to his mouth and was screaming something.

"What?" Ella called out.

A faint reply came: *"Hurry up!"*

"I *am* hurrying up!" Ella yelled. To herself, she added, "I'm just hurrying in all the wrong places."

Something suddenly slammed into her backside and jerked her forward, and Ella was swept into the air. She came back down only to spring forward again, the ground whizzing past her feet. When she saw furry limbs protruding out from under her arms, she realized what was happening. Punchy had picked her up and was carrying her. Ella had enough experience with the Secret Zoo to know he intended to take her to her friends.

"Easy!" Ella said as she was bounced around. "Be careful!"

Punchy dodged a series of tents and leaped across fireless fire pits. Each time he touched down, Ella's shins struck the ground and pain spiked across her knees. The crown of her head was pressed against the kangaroo's long jaw, and Punchy's whiskers repeatedly brushed across her face.

"Slow down!" Ella commanded. "You're scrambling my brains!"

The kangaroo ignored her and continued to cross the forested landscape in massive bounds. Each time he jumped, he reached higher than five feet and sailed forward more than ten yards.

As Punchy rounded a batch of trees, he came upon a large herd of his companions huddled around a sprawling tent. Rather than go around the obstacles, he jumped onto a picnic table and then soared upward with a thrust of his hind legs. Ella let loose a scream as her dangling toes skipped off the canvas crest of the roof, and a second later the duo touched down on the opposite side of the tent, away from the herd.

"Are you nuts!" Ella yelled. "You are *not* a bird!"

Punchy continued on. He steered around tents and trees, dodged signs, and plowed through kangaroos, his powerful legs hammering the ground. The blinking light came into full view, and a minute later they reached the end of the sector, where Tameron and the other scouts stood by. Instead of stopping to let Ella off, Punchy plunged into the final portal and delivered the two of them across the magical divide into the City of Species.

❦ CHAPTER 4 ❧

TARSIER TERRACE

In the City of Species, buildings loomed above the streets. Made of stone, marble, steel, and glass, they seemed a potpourri of architectural designs. Water spilled down their fronts, and trees limbs braced their walls. Animals clung to their façades and dangled from their decorative eaves. Sidewalks reached from their entrances and carved passages to new spots. Noah spotted the octagon-shaped Library of the Secret Society, the vast glass walls of the Wotter Tower, and the bulky mass of the Secret Metr-APE-olis. He smiled, thinking of earlier adventures. In just a few weeks, he'd experienced so much in the magical world a few steps beyond his own backyard.

Animals crowded the streets. Lions rolled their heads and sent waves through their sensuous manes. Running cheetahs blurred their spots, and elephants heaved their pillarlike legs. Birds punched through treetops and streaked color across a boundless canopy of leaves. Fish churned the water in fountains and concrete riverbeds.

"It's good to be back," Megan said as she scanned the treetops, her pigtails resting on her shoulders.

An elephant walked over to the scouts, lifted its trunk, and poked Ella in her stomach.

Ella swatted the strange appendage away, saying, "Hey! Go stick that thing somewhere else! I'm not a jumbo peanut, you know!"

The elephant blinked its eyes, clomped a foot, and trumpeted. It reluctantly stepped back, its ears flapping like two sails of a boat.

The scouts' animal friends appeared from the crowded streets and gathered around them: Blizzard, Little Bighorn, Podgy, and P-Dog and his rowdy coterie of prairie dogs. Blizzard sniffed Noah's extended palm—a greeting the two of them had taken on—and lowered his body to the ground. Noah climbed onto the big polar bear, and Richie took the seat behind him. Ella and Megan mounted Little Bighorn, Ella in the forward spot of their rhinoceros ride. A malachite kingfisher swept down from the crowded treetops and perched on Noah's shoulder. Marlo.

"What's up, buddy?" Noah asked, his head cocked to one side to stare at the tiny blue bird.

Marlo snapped his orange bill toward Noah, chirped once, then looked away.

To the animals, Tameron said, "All right, guys, let's head for Tarsier Terrace. Darby's waiting for us there."

"Tarsier Terrace?" Ella said as Little Bighorn followed the Descender into the street. "Let me guess. A terrace where two hundred gazillion tarsiers hang out."

Tameron ducked beneath the stomach of a giraffe and said, "Yep. Cool little spot, actually. It's where the tarsiers train."

"For perimeter patrol?" Noah asked.

"You guys are catching on."

Tameron led the animals down the street. They passed one side of the Sector of Descent, the place the Descenders lived, and headed down a narrow alley. Here the walls were covered with frogs, bright colors warning of their poison. Blue, red, orange, and yellow, they dotted the stone heights like the splatterings of paint balls. The Crossers emerged at the end of the alley and entered a building. Inside, people bustled about, their attention on clipboards and one another. This seemed to be the place they worked. They couldn't have cared less that a bunch of kids were riding animals through the workplace. Another ordinary sight, here in the Secret Zoo.

"Who are they?" Richie asked Tameron.

"Scientists and research specialists. They develop food."

"Food?"

"Synthetic food. For the predatory animals. We can't have animals eating one another. It sort of defeats our whole purpose of conservation."

"So the animals are protected?" Megan asked.

"Most. But plants and insects, some fish—they're pretty much fair game, as long as they're not threatened in your world."

At the far side of the building, Tameron led the group through two big doors onto an outdoor terrace. Made of decorative stone, the terrace stretched out in both directions and followed the turns of the outside wall. Blizzard and Little Bighorn plodded up to a stone railing, and the scouts stared out over a steep hillside that overlooked a city street at least fifty yards below. Trees grew from the grassy slope and reached far above, their leafy branches stretching across the terrace.

Dozens of tables and chairs were neatly arranged around them. People sat sipping from cups and reading papers. At one table were two men. The first had rocky arms, mountainous shoulders, and a gleaming bald head.

The other had a bushy beard, bushy eyebrows, and long gray hair pulled back in a ponytail. Tank and Mr. Darby. Tank wore a tight leather jacket; Mr. Darby, a long velvet trench coat. Tank had one hand buried in a bag of unshelled peanuts.

"Scouts!" Mr. Darby said as he rose to his feet. He gestured to the open chairs at the table. "Please, please."

The scouts slid down their animal rides and took seats at the table. Tank greeted them in his normal way: a light fist bump with his big ball of knuckles. Podgy waddled up to the table, and Blizzard dropped to his rear end between Ella and Megan. Richie lifted P-Dog onto his lap. Tameron dropped his backpack, leaned against the stone rail, and stared down at the group from the shadow of his hat's short, crooked brim.

Richie, forever hungry as Richie was, leaned across the table and eyed Tank's snack. "What are you eating?"

Tank smiled. Taking the hint, he dumped a pile of peanuts in the middle of the table. "Help yourselves, kiddos."

Richie sang in a high note, "Sweeeetttt!" and then swept up a handful.

A warm grin spread across Mr. Darby's face. He adjusted his sunglasses and said, "I suppose Tameron has told you why I'm here to talk to you."

"Something about you guys needing to rent out our tree fort," Ella said.

"Indeed," the old man said. "It's vital that we keep a more watchful eye on the east side of the zoo, where Tank discovered the sasquatch tracks. To do so, we'd like to move a Descender to Fort Scout, which has a prominent view over the grounds. It's a perfect spot, so dark that there's virtually no risk of a Descender being seen."

The scouts traded glances, unsure of this.

"Consider the sasquatches," Mr. Darby said. "One has found its way into the Grottoes. Think of what it might do to your neighborhood if we permit it to escape. Think of the lives we'd put at risk. This is bigger than the safety of the Secret Zoo—this is the immediate safety of your world, your mothers and fathers."

The scouts had no response to this. They all knew Mr. Darby was right.

"Can we help?" Noah asked. "In the tree fort?"

Tameron stepped up. "Hold up! Let's not get—"

The old man held his hand up to Tameron. "I don't suppose it would hurt for the scouts to check in once and again."

Tameron backed away, clearly a bit miffed.

Everyone stayed silent. Richie crushed a shell in his hand and tossed a nut into his mouth. Seeing this, P-Dog jumped onto the tabletop, scampered across it, and sniffed the pile of peanuts. He grabbed a shell, sat up on his haunches, and held it to his nose.

"It's a nut," Richie explained. "It's something you can eat." He grabbed another shell and demonstrated.

P-Dog studied Richie. Then he sniffed the shell again, bit into its corner, and chewed.

Mr. Darby said, "We'd also like to post an animal."

Noah said, "You're joking, right?"

Mr. Darby shook his head. "A smaller one. And one that can move quickly to the Clarksville Zoo. We think it prudent to keep an animal as a backup to communications. What if a Descender's headset should fail? Or what if a Descender should become injured?"

"But animals . . . how would you get them into Fort Scout?"

"Simple. A branch from the tunnels that run beneath your neighborhood. Or the Grottoes. We've already prepared for this."

The scouts stayed silent again. After a bit, Noah said, "Man . . . we are going to have to be sooo careful."

"Indeed," Mr. Darby said. "Fortunately, we have experience in this area. Think of how long we've been secretly watching your neighborhood."

Noah could say nothing to this.

Smiling, the old man added, "Just like we're secretly watching you—right at this moment."

Richie jolted and snapped a peanut shell into several pieces. "Huh?"

"You're being watched this very instant, in the full light of day, and you've had no idea."

The scouts shared a half-nervous glance, then looked around, high and low.

"The trees," Tank said. He crammed a wad of unshelled peanuts into his mouth and quickly crunched them to pieces. "Look real close in the trees."

The scouts peered out. The branches reached across the long concrete balcony, dangling their colorful leaves above chairs and tables. Noah didn't see a single animal in them.

"I don't see anything," Noah said.

"Me either," said Megan.

Tank winked at Mr. Darby and crammed a few more peanuts into his mouth.

"Keep looking," Mr. Darby said. "But more carefully."

Noah spotted something in a tree. Two round eyes staring out. An animal. It was very small—Noah could have cupped it in his hands—and furry. It had upturned ears and eyes that were huge in proportion to its body. Like a miniature koala, it clung to a branch with all four of its feet. It was so perfectly still that it looked like a bump along the branch.

"I see it," Noah said as he pointed.

The other scouts searched the area beyond the tip of his finger and found it.

"There are more," Mr. Darby said. "Keep looking."

Noah saw a second one. A third. Then more and more, one right after another. They were everywhere in the trees, their bulbous eyes fixed on the scouts.

"Are they tarsiers?" Megan asked.

"Yes," Mr. Darby said. "They're the animals that stake out your neighborhood."

Seeing how small and still the animals were, Noah understood why. In the dark trees of his neighborhood, they were surely at no risk of being seen.

"What are they?" Megan asked. "I've never seen them in the Clarksville Zoo."

It was Richie who answered. "They're from the Philippines, where they risk extinction. They're nocturnal animals with incredible eyesight. And they're arboreal. Sticky pads on their fingers allow them to cling to things. Their hind legs are *waaay* powerful—they can jump like five feet high and twenty feet long. They're like a cross between kangaroos and frogs."

"Amazing," Ella said as she looked at Richie. "Your brain . . . it's like the world's smallest database."

Richie shrugged. "Knowledge is what I do."

Tank said, "My little man's right. Tarsiers can see a long way at night. And they can hear just about everything. They're perfect for our patrols."

Ella said, "I can't decide if they're cute or creepy."

Noah turned back to one of the tarsiers. With its big round eyes and dotlike pupils, it looked cute and kind and terrified, all at the same time. It had its stare locked on the scouts.

Mr. Darby chuckled. "They certainly are unusual creatures! And to think . . . we post hundreds in your trees at night. And no one suspects a thing!"

Megan said, "It's still so hard to believe. All these tunnels around our houses . . . And animals in our trees!"

A tarsier suddenly moved out along a branch just above the scouts' heads. It crawled like a squirrel, its long fingers clinging to the bark. It stopped about fifteen feet from the table and fixed its wild, bug-eyed stare directly at Richie. Blizzard craned his neck toward the strange animal and sniffed its scent out of the air.

"Uh-oh," Ella said with a smile. "Did Richie find a new friend?"

Richie, who'd just dropped a fresh load of peanuts into his mouth, tensed in his chair and nervously watched the tarsier. "Why is he looking at me like that?" he mumbled through his full mouth. "And why does he look ready to pounce?"

"Relax, Richie," Ella said with a chuckle. "Why are you always so worried? It's not like that thing can—"

The tarsier sprang off the branch, leaving it trembling. It soared fifteen feet through the air and touched down on Richie's head. Biting and pulling, it attacked the pom-pom on his cap. Richie screamed and sprayed bits of peanuts everywhere, dotting Tank's and Mr. Darby's jackets. On the tabletop, P-Dog panicked as well. He ran in circles and then dove toward the ground, but not before claiming a shelled peanut in his mouth for a later snack.

"GET IT OFF!" Richie screamed.

The tarsier jerked its head in all directions, its sharp teeth buried in the tuft of threads. It kicked its hind legs against Richie's head as it tried to uproot the pom-pom.

Marlo sprang off Noah's shoulder, flew at the tarsier, and pecked its furry behind with his sharp beak. The tarsier dove back to the branch, then disappeared into the trees. Richie, white as the polar bear beside him, fell back into his chair and clutched his chest, gasping for breath.

"Well," Mr. Darby said as he brushed chewed-up peanuts off his velvet jacket with an obvious air of disgust. "That was certainly . . . most unusual."

"You mean for Richie?" Ella asked. "Naw . . . he always acts that way."

"I'm speaking of the tarsier."

"Apparently not a big fan of pom-poms," Ella said.

"He must have thought it was an insect," Mr. Darby said. "Insects . . . that's what they eat."

P-Dog stood on his haunches beside Richie's chair and yipped up at his friend. Richie squinted down and chided him, saying, "Nice work, P. Glad you had my back on that one." Looking offended, P-Dog yipped a second time and then hastened off.

Noah, a smile still on his face, turned back to the trees. He scanned the branches and searched for the tarsiers again. Their faint brown color blended their bodies into their surroundings. But Noah could see their eyes—hundreds of them staring out.

"What do they do here?" Noah asked. "At Tarsier Terrace, I mean."

"Would you like to see?" said Mr. Darby. The old man pushed away from the table and walked to the stone rail along the edge of the terrace. The entire group followed, even the animals. Through a large opening in the trees, they stared down on the busy city streets.

"What are we looking for?" Megan asked.

"*We* are not looking for anything. It's the tarsiers that are looking for something. They're training—that's what they do here."

Noah looked around and realized the tarsiers had their bulbous eyes turned away from the scouts and toward the streets below.

A few minutes passed. Then a few more. Nothing happened.

Ella said, "What in the world are—"

"Patience, dear Ella," Mr. Darby said.

The scouts' animal friends began to get bored. The prairie dogs started chasing a dry leaf around. Little Bighorn wandered across the terrace, his down-turned snout curiously sweeping over the stone floor. Blizzard lowered himself to his stomach, rested his chin on his paws, and half closed his eyes.

Sometime afterward, a batch of leaves off to their left began to violently shake. A tarsier was rocking a thin limb, heaving his weight up and down, all four of his feet curled around the bark. His bulging eyes were fixed on something on the distant street.

"What's he doing?" Megan asked.

A tiny owl swooped down from the heights and landed beside the tarsier. The big-eyed arboreal animal stopped shaking the branch, and the owl flew off.

"Very nice," Mr. Darby said to Tank. "Very speedy execution."

"Execution?" Richie said. "What are you guys talking about?"

"The tarsier," Mr. Darby said. "It sighted the target and alerted the second layer of surveillance—namely, the owls."

The scouts stared down on the busy city streets, where no fewer than a hundred people and animals were roaming about.

"What target?" Richie said.

"A fedora hat," Tank said. "Like the one DeGraff has

been reported to wear. Anyone see it?"

The scouts continued to look down. The city street was a swirl of color and activity, feathers and fur.

"We're supposed to find a hat in all that?" Richie asked.

Ella said, "Talk about 'Where's Waldo?' "

"There!" Megan said, her arm stretched out. "On that giraffe!"

The scouts leaned over the rail. The hat was somehow attached to the animal's long tail.

Ella pulled her head back on her shoulders and scrunched up her face. "Why in the world is it taped to a giraffe's butt?"

Mr. Darby said, "We train the tarsiers to spot the known details of DeGraff. His hat, his boots, his jacket."

Noah became interested in the owl that had vanished into the trees. "So if this were a real sighting of DeGraff, that owl would alert the Descender at the nearest post, then lead him and a few security guards here."

"Precisely," Mr. Darby said. "Simple, yes?"

Noah nodded. It was.

"Excellent," Mr. Darby said. "On that note, I believe it's time for the four of you to find your way home. Tameron, I trust you can show our young Crossers the door."

Tameron fed his arms into the straps of his backpack and said, "C'mon, kids. Let's go."

The scouts said quick good-byes to their animal

friends—the stroke of a back, the tap of a head, the scratch of a chin—and followed Tameron across the terrace. At the door to the building, Noah swung back and said, "When will you start? Posting a Descender in our fort, I mean."

"This very night," Mr. Darby said.

Noah felt something rise in his chest. Fear? Concern? Were the scouts making the right call in allowing the members of a secret world to hide in Noah's yard at night?

Noah didn't know what to say, so he simply turned and walked off, leaving Tank and Mr. Darby on the strange terrace.

CHAPTER 5

THE LOOKOUT FROM FORT SCOUT

"**A**nyone see anything?" Ella whispered.

The scouts stood in their pajamas at the window in the Nowicki kitchen, staring out at Fort Scout. It was almost midnight, and Noah's parents had been asleep for at least two hours. The backyard was so dark that Noah could only faintly see Fort Scout, a dim rectangle caught in the limbs of the distant oak tree.

"Nuh-uh," said Noah.

After giving permission earlier that day for the Secret Society to post a Descender in their tree fort, the scouts had decided on a sleepover at Noah and Megan's house.

They all wanted to be near the incredible event taking place in Fort Scout—an animal and a teenager from another world keeping watch over the east wall of the zoo.

"Me neither," said Richie. He wore footed pajamas, and even indoors he had on his winter hat with the bushy pom-pom. Simulating a yawn, he stretched his arms above his head and added, "It sure is getting late. Well, better hit the sack, I guess!"

Ignoring Richie, Ella asked the other two, "You think they're even out there?"

Megan and Noah shrugged.

Ella hoisted her rear end onto the counter and peered out the window, cupping her hands around her eyes to reduce the glare of the kitchen lights.

"Anything?" Noah asked.

"No way. Too dark."

They continued to stare out. After a few minutes, Megan had the courage to say what Noah was thinking. "Let's go out there."

They shared a glance, silently wondering if this was possible.

Richie waved his hands at them, saying, "I'm thinking that's *not* such a good idea. I'm sure Mrs. Nowicki would just love to wake up and find us running around the yard in our pj's."

"She won't," said Noah. "Besides, if she does, we'll just tell her that Megan lost her glasses in Fort Scout again."

The three scouts stared at Richie, whose eyes darted nervously among them. "I think I see what's going on here. All the stress . . . it has Play-Doh'ed your brains!"

The others said nothing.

"Okay," said Richie, "let's disregard our emotions." His posture stiffened as he began to intellectualize. "Let's regard this from a logical standpoint. Let's assume—"

But the three scouts were already at the back door, slipping on their hats and jackets and stepping into their shoes. Within seconds, they were fully dressed, and Megan eased open the back door, trying to quiet the squeal of the hinges.

Richie whispered angrily, "Guys—don't be stupid!"

Ignoring him, the other scouts exited. They were halfway to the tree fort when Richie finally gave up and rushed after them, calling in a hoarse whisper for his friends to wait up.

Outside, it was winter cold. The wind ushered clouds across the sky. Thick and billowy, they seemed strong enough to catch falling stars. A bit of snow colored the grass.

The four friends raced up the ladder to Fort Scout, and Noah pushed open the door, revealing not two but three figures huddled near the window: Podgy, Marlo, and Hannah. Hannah was one of the four Descenders assigned to perimeter patrol. She had wild blond hair with red bangs and was endlessly chewing gum. She wore magical platform boots that allowed her to jump like a puma—her Descender power. Podgy and Hannah were on the floor, and Marlo was perched on the window frame.

The scouts rushed inside and gathered around the Secret Cityzens, taking seats on the cold wooden planks. Marlo dove through the air and found his usual perch on Noah's shoulder.

Hannah's jaw dropped open. "What are you doing out here?"

"We just wanted to see how things are going," Megan explained.

"And get us spotted?"

Noah reassured her. "My parents are asleep. And we could barely see Fort Scout from the window anyway."

Megan said, "We'll only stay for a little bit. We promise!"

"If Sam knew you guys were already—" Hannah cut herself short, her stare fixed on Richie's feet. "Are those footsie pajamas?"

Richie smiled. "Yeppers."

Hannah shook her head. "Great. The fate of the world rests on a kid who dresses like an infant." Frowning, she

gazed around at the scouts. "You can stay a half hour—
not a second more."

"Awesome!" said Ella.

Looking at Podgy, Megan asked, "How did he get in
here?"

Hannah said, "His wings work now, remember?" She
gestured out the tree fort. "And the zoo's right there. All
he had to do was get over the wall. The stairs to the fort
made the rest easy."

Noah peered out. From twenty-five feet high, he could
see easily over the concrete wall, which skirted his property line and ran along his neighbors' yards to finally disappear behind the trees. The otherworldly zoo landscape,
dimly lit by scattered lamps, was especially wondrous at
night. Silhouettes of concrete mountainsides rose against
a starry backdrop, and great dome roofs loomed. Naked
tree branches reached skyward, as if trying to cover
themselves with the falling moonlight.

Peering out the window next to Noah, Megan said, "With
the leaves off the trees, you can see so many exhibits."

She was right. Noah quickly counted thirty. Not far
from them was the sprawl of multipurpose igloos in
Arctic Town. In the distance rose the Forest of Flight,
Penguin Palace, and Metr-APE-olis. In Rhinorama, Little
Bighorn, draped in darkness, ambled along the exhibit's
grassy perimeter.

Everyone became quiet. Time passed. The view—tranquil and familiar—softened Noah's mood. He glanced at the others: Richie with his footed pajamas, Ella with her fluffy pink earmuffs, Megan with her drooping pigtails. Being with them in the tree fort, he suddenly felt a welcome distance from the rest of the world. He was with his best friends, the family beyond his own.

Richie yanked him out of his feelings, saying, "Guys—did you see—"

"I saw it!" said Ella. "Something's out there!"

"Just police-monkeys," Hannah calmly said. "On patrol."

Noah snatched up a pair of binoculars. Two houses down, the limbs of a tree shifted, then a small branch broke off and dropped to the ground. Two monkeys became visible. They leaped and swung through the branches, making their way to the house. They dropped down on the roof, where they scurried to a gabled peak and ducked into the shadows of a chimney.

Megan looked at Noah. "See," she said. "Told you."

"Huh?"

"Monkeys on the rooftops," Megan said. "When all this started, I told you, and you didn't believe me."

"Oh," Noah said. "Yeah—sorry about that."

The scouts fell silent and watched the rooftop. The monkeys sat facing the zoo, their backs against the chimney. Behind them, a plume of colorless smoke spilled skyward. Every so often, a monkey swung its head to scan the surroundings.

"Look at them," said Ella. "It's just crazy."

Seconds later, the monkeys sprang to their feet and ran in the opposite direction of the scouts. They jumped off the roof, sailed through the air, then touched down on the next house, where they ran to its gabled peak and once again tucked themselves into the cover of a chimney. There they scanned the landscape for a few minutes before standing, running to the edge of the house, and pitching themselves into the air once more. They landed on the next rooftop and headed across it, their figures dissolving into the darkness.

The scouts turned to Hannah with blank expressions. She brushed back her wild red bangs and said, "No biggie. They're just doing what they're supposed to."

The four friends shared a bewildered look and then returned their attention to the zoo. For the next fifteen minutes, nothing unusual happened. Occasional guards strolled the grounds, and animals paced their yards, making Noah remember something Tameron had said during their first crosstraining: "The Secret Zoo has two lines of defense, one of humans and one of animals." Certainly those two lines were what the scouts were seeing now.

Just as Noah was about to ask his friends if they wanted

to go back into the house, a bat darted past, its wings slicing through the darkness.

"You guys see that?" Richie asked. "The bat—it was patrolling."

"How do you know it wasn't just an ordinary bat?" Ella asked.

"Ordinary bats hibernate this time of year," Richie answered. "Again I present the rewards of staying awake in class."

Ella twisted her face and stared hard at her friend. "Keep it up, and I'll present my fist."

A second bat appeared. Then another, and another, each spaced perhaps thirty feet behind the previous one. Unlike the smooth, graceful sweeps with which most birds flew, the bats jerked across the sky, zigzagging from one point to the next. They seemed to be on parade, the moon and stars their only known audience.

The scouts watched, their faces turned upward. Marlo sidestepped back and forth across Noah's shoulder, his beady eyes fixed on the bats. Podgy watched, too. As many as twenty bats darted past before the sky settled and the only movement again became the steady, wind-driven passage of the clouds.

The scouts turned back at the zoo. A few minutes went by. Noah remembered the tarsiers and peered into the neighborhood trees.

"I don't see any tarsiers," he said.

"That's why this whole thing works," Hannah answered.

Her weighty tone suggested she was tiring of the scouts' questions and remarks. Sensing this, Noah told his friends they should probably go. As he turned to Podgy, Marlo jumped from his shoulder and landed on the window.

"See you later, Podge," said Noah.

In acknowledgment, Podgy flapped his flippers once.

Noah turned to Hannah, who was crouched beside the window. She had faint streaks of moonlight in her wild hair.

"See you," he said.

Hannah nodded. "Don't wake up your mom."

The scouts rode the slide to the ground. They quickly crossed the backyard and slipped into the house, where Noah's parents slept, oblivious to the threats around them. In the living room, the scouts squirmed into their sleeping bags. They closed their eyes, and no one spoke. They all knew they needed their sleep if they were going to protect their neighborhood from the mounting dangers of the Secret Zoo.

CHAPTER 6

An Instant Marlo

After dinner on Sunday, the scouts lounged in their tree fort. On the floor, Megan and Ella were stretched out on their backs, their heads resting in their hands. Richie was at the table, probing at the electrical remains of a long-dead gadget, his hopes set on resurrecting it. Noah was staring out the window toward the zoo. As evening began to dim the day, a tiny blue bird streaked through the window and touched down on Noah's shoulder.

"Marlo!" Richie called out.

The scouts jumped to attention. Noah took a seat on the floor, and his friends huddled near him. In Marlo's beak was a folded slip of paper, a message from someone in the Secret Society, likely Mr. Darby. The scouts called these messages IMs—Instant Marlos. Noah plucked the note from Marlo's beak, opened it, then read it out loud.

> *Dearest Scouts,*
> *Due to the recent sasquatch sighting outside the inner borders of the Clarksville Zoo, Tank and I would like to divert the focus of your crosstraining to the Grottoes. Please reply if you can meet Tank in Butterfly Nets tomorrow after school. More will be explained then.*
> *Best wishes,*
> *Mr. Darby*

"The Grottoes?" Megan said. "Things sure have changed, huh?"

The other scouts knew what she was referring to. Up to this point, the four of them had been warned to keep out of the Grottoes—to use only tunnels that opened directly to the Secret Zoo. Noah had once ventured into the Grottoes, got lost in the exhibits, and been nearly spotted by zoo visitors. The Descenders had been furious.

"Yep," Ella said. "Looks like they might be rethinking their defense strategy. Guess that happens once sasquatches start shopping in your gift shops."

Noah snatched a pen from Richie's pocket, flattened the letter against the floor, and wrote, "We'll be there." He folded the paper back into a tiny square, then held it up to Marlo, who plucked it free with a peck of his beak. The kingfisher dove into the air and flashed out of sight.

They traded glances, each trying to read the emotions coded in one another's stares.

"The Grottoes?" asked Ella.

"The Grottoes," answered Noah.

"Here we go," said Megan.

"Oh boy," Richie said.

⚜ CHAPTER 7 ⚜
EXPLORING THE GROTTOES

fter school on Monday, the scouts stood at the entrance to Butterfly Nets beside the "CLOSED FOR CONSTRUCTION!" sign. Noah pulled the magic key from his pocket. He looked left, then right, then jabbed the key at the slot in the door. The lock clicked open, and one by one the scouts slipped inside. They were greeted by Tank. The mountainous man stood with his arms crossed, his bald head gleaming. His chest bulged out like the shells of two turtles.

"What's up?" Tank asked. He fist-tapped the scouts, then said to Noah, "Lead the way, bub. You know how to get into the Grottoes from here."

Noah blushed with shame. Tank was referring to how Noah had sneaked into the Grottoes from this exhibit not long ago. Though Noah doubted Tank was holding a grudge against him, he couldn't help but feel a bit guilty.

Butterfly Nets was a long glass house with a gabled rooftop. An open exhibit, it was full of trees, plants, streams, and noisy waterfalls. Hundreds of butterflies flitted from spot to spot, flashing color onto the surroundings. Meshed rope was draped all around to look like large nets.

Noah walked down the visitor path, slipped under a railing, then ventured into the restricted part of the exhibit, ducking branches and crossing streams. He led the group around a fabricated rock formation to a hidden spot. A narrow flight of stairs descended into the ground. The Crossers took them.

The dark staircase landing opened in one direction. When Noah stepped that way, a series of lights triggered on. Richie yelped, and Ella shushed him. A short tunnel headed straight for ten feet and then stopped at two branches, one left and one right. The group moved forward and stared down both passages. As much as fifty feet long, each had five or six new branches—mouths to new tunnels. The entrances were cloaked with velvet curtains.

"Is this it?" Ella asked.

"Part of it," Tank replied. "But the Grottoes . . . they're

big." He squeezed through the four of them and headed down the branch to the right. "This way."

Old bricks shaped the walls and arched ceiling. Flecks of mortar peppered the edges of the dirt floor. Above each curtain was a gold plate with words engraved upon it. The first plate read "A-Lotta-Hippopotami." The second, "Ostrich Island."

Tank said, "Take a seat for a sec. I'm about to school you in the Grottoes."

The scouts dropped to their bottoms and leaned back against the cool wall.

Sliding his palms together, Tank began to slowly pace in front of the scouts, assuming the traditional posture of a lecturer quite naturally.

"The Grottoes are nothing but a bunch of ordinary tunnels running beneath the Clarksville Zoo. They're on the fringes of the Secret Zoo, but they're most certainly *not* in it. The Grottoes have gateways." Tank touched the curtain behind him. "Portals. These are magical, as you know. Sometimes they connect to sectors in the Secret Zoo. Sometimes they connect to places in the Clarksville Zoo, exhibits and other spots—spots like this. . . ." Tank tapped his knuckles against the gold plate above the curtain beside him. It read "Grottoes ENE." "Anyone know how to read a compass?" When Richie stabbed his arm into the air, Tank asked, "Tell me what *ENE* stands for."

"East-northeast," Richie said.

Tank winked. "You got it. A compass has four cardinal points—north, south, east, and west. In the middle of any two cardinal points are intercardinal points—northeast, southeast, places like that. And then you have secondary intercardinal points—north-northeast, west-southeast. Makes for a total of sixteen points."

"And makes me glad we upgraded compasses to satellites," Ella added.

"This tunnel"—Tank again touched the plate that read "Grottoes ENE"—"this connects to the east-northeast end of the Grottoes."

"That's right by my house," Noah said.

"Yep. Pretty close. And from there you can gate to other ends of the Grottoes, places in the Clarksville Zoo, and sectors in the Secret Zoo."

Ella said, "What's up with all these crazy tunnels? I mean, why not just have straight drops to the Secret Zoo and get around places in the Clarksville Zoo from aboveground?"

"Not fast enough," Tank said. "And too visible to Outsiders."

"But—"

"Hold on, let me explain. In the first years of the Clarksville Zoo, we had nothing but straight drops to the Secret Zoo. The Grottoes . . . they didn't exist. But once

DeGraff breached our borders, we started protecting them. Animals watched over the portals in their exhibits, and security guards patrolled the Clarksville Zoo grounds. Most important, we assembled the first team of human Crossers.

"For a while, it was enough to put the Secret Cityzens at ease. But then the Sasquatch Rebellion went down. Hundreds were killed. Parts of the City of Species were destroyed. Things fell apart for us. Attitudes changed. Focus was lost, and fear became our government. The Descenders were born, and they quickly emerged as our army. Most were descendants of people killed in the attack. They engineered a way to take the magic into themselves, then to our borders. The first tunnels in the Grottoes were created, and they had but one purpose: to quickly move the Descenders to different points in the two zoos."

It pained Noah to hear how violence had helped shape the marvel of the Secret Zoo.

"Using the Grottoes, the Descenders can respond to an attack in the Secret Zoo, or a sighting of DeGraff in the Clarksville Zoo, within minutes, sometimes seconds. Using the portals, they literally jump from place to place."

To the scouts' left, the bottom of a curtain suddenly flapped open. Dozens of meerkats charged into the Grottoes. They ran over and under the scouts' legs, then disappeared through another curtain at the far end of the tunnel.

"Like those guys?" Richie asked.

"Pretty much," said Tank.

Ella pointed to where the meerkats had gone, saying, "You know your life has hit a record for weirdness when something like *that* seems perfectly normal."

Richie swung his stare back to Tank and said, "How did they build the Grottoes?"

"First they developed a layout that made sense. Then everyone went to work. Old-fashioned muscle created the tunnels; the brothers created the portals."

Noah looked around him at the stone walls and velvet curtains. He thought of the brothers Tank had mentioned—Bhanu, Kavi, and Vishal, three identical brothers from India, born to different mothers. When joined together, they could work magic, and it had been their magic that had helped create the Secret Zoo.

"Well . . ." Tank added, "the brothers created most of the portals, anyway."

"Most?" Noah said. "What do you mean by that?"

Tank paused and seemed to look inward. Finally, he said, "Before the Grottoes could be completed, one of the brothers died. Kavi. Old age got him. We buried him in one of the sectors. Without Kavi, the magic of the surviving brothers weakened. The farther the two of them were from their brother's gravesite, the weaker their magic was.

"Vishal died several years later. Another natural death. The Secret Society buried him close to his brother. Bhanu's magic became weaker than ever. He could barely do anything unless he was near his brothers' graves.

"Finally, a few years later, age got the best of Bhanu. We buried him in the same sector as his brothers . . . and that was that."

Ella said, "Why do I have a feeling that something bad happened?"

"Something did," Tank said. "The portals stopped working."

"All of them?"

"Not from the City of Species to the sectors—just from the sectors to the outside world, the ones that require more magic."

"But obviously you guys fixed it," Megan said. "How?"

"An act of desperation. When the brothers were alive, their magic only worked when they were together. Wondering if the same was true in their death, we unburied them and put them in a single casket. When we did, the portals to your world started working again."

"The Cemetery Sector . . ." Noah said in a hushed voice. He knew that the Cemetery Sector was one of the Forbidden Five, five sectors that were off-limits to all except a select few. "That's where they're buried, right?"

Tank nodded.

"Cool!" Ella said. "Can we check it out?"

"Not a chance," Tank shot back. "That place . . . it's filled with too much magic. It wouldn't be safe. The Cemetery Sector is . . ." Tank clearly couldn't find the right words. "Let's just say it's like nothing you've ever seen."

The scouts thought about this. After a bit, Noah said, "When we first found the Secret Zoo, Mr. Darby told us the magic was still alive, and that you guys still use it."

Tank nodded. "That's where our magical scientists come in. For years, they've been working in the Cemetery Sector, studying the magic and discovering ways to use it. They've gotten pretty good at it. They can't create sectors, but they can modify them."

"The Secret Wotter Park!" Megan said. "It's inside a water tower in the City of Species. I remember Hannah telling us that it was the result of a consolidation project—something to open up space in one of the sectors."

"Yep," Tank said. "Our scientists did that. Nice job, huh?"

"I want to hang out with these scientist dudes," Ella said. Then her stare went blank as she wandered off into her own thoughts. "Yeah . . . I bet we could do some *really* wicked stuff."

Tank switched the conversation back, saying, "There's a science and a structure to the magic. A math. Once the scientists found its logic, they went to work creating portals. They did most of their testing in Kangaroo Kampground. You guys just crosstrained there, so you know what I'm talking about."

The scouts nodded enthusiastically.

"The scientists created a ton of the minor portals in the Grottoes. And even though they're good with the magic, they're still not Bhanu and his brothers. Some of the portals in the Grottoes are"—Tank's voice trailed off as he tried to select the right words—"a bit less than perfect."

"Uh-oh . . ." Richie said. "What do you mean by that?"

"Sometimes they don't portal to the right spots. And sometimes they don't portal at all. Other times"—Tank's voice trailed off again—"other times Crossers don't make it through."

The scouts flinched. Richie clutched his chest.

"What happens to them?" Ella asked.

Tank shook his head, looking sad. "We don't know. They disappear. For good. We call it 'going amiss.'"

"Oh nice!" Ella said. "And a few days ago, Noah was running through them like they're the best part of a funhouse!"

Tank shrugged his shoulders. "We told you guys to stay out of the Grottoes."

"But you guys know which portals are dangerous, right?"

Tank stayed silent for what seemed a very long time. "We know some that are."

"You know *some*?" Richie barked. "Didn't you guys pay attention to which ones the scientists created?"

With some shame in his voice, Tank said, "What can I say—details sometimes get lost in history!"

"Great," Ella said. "Nice record-keeping, guys."

Noah asked, "How often do people . . . *go amiss?*"

"Almost never," Tank said. "Try not to sweat it. You have a better chance of getting struck by lightning."

The scouts slowly shook their heads. As always, the story of the Secret Zoo was almost too much to believe. Noah turned to his friends. Ella's jaw was open, and Richie's fingertips were pressed to the sides of his head. Megan's eyes were almost as big as the lenses in her glasses.

"Tank?" Noah said. "Something doesn't make sense."

"What's that, bub?"

"If Bhanu and his brothers died of old age, why didn't DeGraff?"

Tank frowned. "He's not human anymore—not the way his brothers were. Something happened to him on the day he used his magic to draw the shadows into himself. Some say he's now nothing but a dark swarm of energy. Others say he's part shadow and part human. Others admit they have no idea what he is. Most . . . most don't even believe he exists anymore. They figure he died along with his brothers. They see him as a legend, a myth. They're always asking, if he's still alive, why he hasn't attacked the Clarksville Zoo after so many years."

The scouts traded uneasy glances.

"Okay," Tank said with some finality. He turned toward the curtain and pulled one side open. "You guys ready to explore?"

"Yeah," Ella said. "Just not so ready to go amiss."

Tank grinned and said, "Try not to think about it. Like I said—it almost never happens."

As the scouts followed the big man through the portal marked "Grottoes ENE," Noah hoped not to end up in some strange and forgotten place beyond the world of the Secret Zoo.

ఆ CHAPTER 8 ్య

Below the Knickknack
and Snack Shack

The scouts stepped out into a new tunnel that looked very much like the other. Stone walls rose more than ten feet above them, and the ceiling was arched. Velvet curtains dangled in front of dark passageways. Up ahead, the tunnel swung left and disappeared. A few dim lights were set in the walls. Insects skittered across the floor, and dusty cobwebs clung to corners. The eerie underground passage reminded Noah of something beneath an ancient city.

"The Grottoes," Tank said. "East-northeast side of the zoo."

An earthy, musty smell hung about, and the stale air was difficult to breathe. Noah stroked his fingertips across the walls; they were damp and cool and gritty.

"East-northeast's been here a long time," Tank said. He'd turned around and was now walking backward in order to face the scouts. "It's an original section—no going amiss here."

As they walked past the curtains, Richie read the engravings on the gold plates out loud: "'The Secret Koala Kastle' . . . 'Metr-APE-olis' . . . 'The Secret Chinchillavilla' . . ."

Tank said, "All the ones marked 'secret' go to sectors in the Secret Zoo. All the others go to places in the Clarksville Zoo—mostly exhibits, but a few ordinary sites, too."

Noah remembered his sneaky visit to the Grottoes and how he'd ended up in Flamingo Fountain. He knew a thing or two about the "ordinary sites" Tank was referring to. They were hardly ordinary when you emerged in them on the back of an emperor penguin.

The walls around a curtain marked "The Secret Elephant Event" began to rumble. The ceiling rained dirt and powdery pieces of mortar. The ground shook, and insects scattered. Richie, who'd been standing in front of the curtain, jumped out of the way, ducking behind Ella. From where Noah stood, it looked like Ella's head had suddenly sprouted the pom-pom on Richie's cap.

Tank laughed. "Don't sweat it, Richie. The elephants

are just goofing around. Happens all the time. They won't come into the Grottoes unless they need to."

The rumble softened and then faded out altogether as the elephant charged off into the reaches of the sector.

Tank dropped down beside a curtain marked "The Knickknack and Snack Shack." "Right here," he said as he pointed to the ground.

The scouts crouched low around the big man.

"Here's one of the sasquatch prints I saw."

The impressions in a soft spot in the ground detailed a foot—one that could crush a full-grown watermelon. Richie gasped.

"You got to be kidding me!" Ella said. "You sure it wasn't King Kong strolling around down here?"

"This was a sasquatch," he said. "Medium sized."

"Medium sized!" Richie squeaked. His lips curled into new shapes as he searched for something more to say. In the end, he managed only to squeak, "Medium sized!" a second time.

Tank rose and pulled back the curtain to the Knickknack and Snack Shack. "Follow me."

The scouts did. When the curtain touched Noah, he felt its magic course through him like a weak jolt of electricity. Beyond the gateway, the tunnel continued straight about fifteen feet and ended at a steep flight of blocky steps. Tank headed toward it, a few dim lights in the walls showing the way. Halfway up the stairs, he turned to the scouts, held his finger to the tip of his nose, and emitted a near-silent "Shhhhh. . . ."

"How come?" Richie whispered.

Tank lifted his finger toward the ceiling.

The scouts craned their necks. They listened. Faint footsteps came from above. And a muffled voice. Noah heard something else as well: a muted *ding!*, like that of a cash register.

"The Knickknack and Snack Shack," Megan whispered.

"Up there," Tank mouthed.

Noah had totally forgotten where they really were. Right above them was the Clarksville City Zoo, bustling with activity.

With a sideways nod of his head, Tank gestured for the scouts to continue up the steps. At the top of the staircase was a long hatch door. Tank and the scouts crawled up and hunkered in beneath it. In the shadowy recess, it was almost too dark to see. Tank's big eyes seemed to hover in space like the eyes of a comic strip character startled by the dark. The Crossers were huddled so close that Noah could hear his friends breathing.

"Ugh," Ella softly groaned.

"What's wrong?" Tank whispered.

"I smell someone's breath. Or armpit. Either way, I think I'm going to barf."

"Sorry," Richie whispered. "I had onion rings for lunch. Anyone got a mint?"

"One mint?" Ella said. "You'd have more luck putting out a forest fire with a wet wipe."

As their eyes began to adjust, Noah saw Tank's arm reach out and pluck Richie's penlight from his shirt pocket. He turned it on and shined it along the far end of the hatch.

"See that?" Tank whispered.

Several strong hinges were fastened to the edge of the hatch. Along one was a tuft of mangy hair.

"Sasquatch left that," Tank whispered. "Got its fur pinched in it."

The scouts stared at the tuft of hair, silent.

Above them the cash register dinged again. Then footsteps moved across the hatch.

"Just past this door you can see the east side of the perimeter wall. Fort Scout is clear as day."

Noah thought about this. Then he said, "You think the sasquatches will try to escape here?"

Tank shrugged. "Maybe. Makes sense, don't you think? It's the least-guarded spot in the whole Clarksville Zoo."

In a whisper, Megan said, "But maybe this sasquatch just wandered off. Got lost in the Grottoes before eventually making its way back."

"Could be," Tank said. "But we've seen the sasquatches are smarter than that, haven't we?"

Noah thought of the Dark Lands—how the sasquatches had kept Megan prisoner for weeks knowing the Secret Society would eventually come after her, presenting them a way to escape. Tank was right. The sasquatches might be as smart as humans.

Maybe even smarter.

"C'mon," Tank said as he squeezed by the scouts on his way down the steps. "I got a few more things to show you before we're done for the day."

For the next forty-five minutes, Tank escorted the scouts through the Grottoes, explaining them as they went. By the gateway to the Secret Rhinorama, they heard the muffled sound of a stampede beating through the walls. At the portal to the Secret Penguin Palace, they stroked their hands along a sheet of ice that had formed over the bricks. By an entrance to the Secret Butterfly Nets, they walked through a cloud of butterflies. Near the portal to the Secret Forest of Flight, they kicked though a kaleidoscopic spill of feathers.

Finally, Tank led them to a velvet curtain marked "Zoo Security." To get through, they had to cram themselves into a small room. There was enough light to see that in front of them was a pair of folding doors that opened outward. Noah realized they were in a closet.

Ella said, "You sure we're not about to step into Narnia."

Tank chuckled. "Narnia's make-believe, girl." Then he pushed through.

They walked into a place that Noah immediately realized was the small security building at the front of the
Clarksville Zoo. The building had a wall with long tinted
windows that looked out at the main gates. Another wall
had dozens of black-and-white security monitors mounted
to it. At a desk in front of this wall sat a man with fire-
bright red hair. With his back to Tank and the scouts,
he was thumbing through a magazine and bobbing his
head as an iPod poured music into his ears. When Tank
tapped him on the shoulder, he spun around, revealing a
frightened, freckled face. Charlie Red, one of the scouts'
biggest enemies.

Charlie jumped from his chair. "Tank—you want to
give me a heart attack!"

Tank bellowed laughter and clapped Charlie on the shoulder. "Sorry, man," he said. "Just thought we'd drop by."

"Next time, call first," Charlie said. His gaze wandered
off to the scouts, and he said, "Oh, you brought company."

"Yes, indeed," Tank said. "Just showing our little friends
the ropes."

Charlie considered this. Without taking his eyes off the
scouts, he said, "And you think that's a good idea?"

"Mr. D does," Tank said. "And that's pretty much all
that matters." He turned to the scouts and said, "C'mon,
gang. Time to go home." Then he headed for the nearby
exit.

Charlie leaned toward the scouts, stuck his chest out, and scowled at them as they passed. Richie cowered to one side. But Ella crossed her eyes, stuck out her tongue, and shoved her face right back at him.

Outside, Tank said, "We'll send a message with Marlo to set up the next crosstraining. We'll spend some more time in the Grottoes."

Noah thought of all they had seen today. "What more is there?" he asked.

Tank winked and said, "Oh . . . there's so much more. Why don't we keep it a surprise."

With that, the big man turned and walked back into the security building. The scouts looked at one another and realized the place for words was gone. They turned, headed through the main gates, and made their way home.

CHAPTER 9

QUESTIONS IN FORT SCOUT

Noah fitfully tossed on his bed. He couldn't sleep. His excited mind kept replaying scenes from the scouts' excursion through the Grottoes earlier that day. It kept astounding him to think that the web of tunnels extended into his neighborhood. Did they run through his own yard? If so, were prairie dogs in them this very moment?

Noah unknotted himself from the sheets and jumped out of bed. The clock on his nightstand read 1:36. He went to the window, peered out into the distant trees, and tried to pull the image of a tarsier from the shadowy shapes. Nothing. As usual, there was no sign of the peculiar, bug-eyed things.

His thoughts drifted to Fort Scout. He could hardly believe that his tree fort was being used by citizens of another world to guard the border of his local zoo from an ancient evil. He wondered who was out there. Which Descender? And which animal?

"At what point did my life go so incredibly insane?" he asked himself.

Knowing he wasn't going to be able to sleep any time soon, he snuck out of his bedroom and tiptoed down the hall. He crept down the stairs and into the kitchen. He stared out the window at Fort Scout but could see little more than its basic shape. An idea struck him. It wouldn't hurt to go out and check on everything. Maybe it would help put his mind at ease, and Mr. Darby had said it was okay.

"I'll just peek in," he told himself.

At the back door, he slipped on his jacket and his red hunting cap. He eased himself outside and bolted across the yard, the big earflaps on his cap bouncing. He climbed the ladder and entered the fort. Sitting by a window was Sam, the Descender who used the magic of his jacket to grow wings and fly. Around him were close to a dozen prairie dogs. Sam stared at Noah with a stunned look on his face.

"I couldn't sleep," Noah explained.

"Are you—" Sam glanced toward the house and checked the windows. All the lights were off. "It would be just great if your mom woke up right now and found your bed empty."

"She won't."

"And how do you know that?"

"She's a heavy sleeper. Both my parents are." Noah paused. "Listen, I'm not going to stay long. I just want to see what you're doing. Besides . . . it *is* my tree fort, you know."

Sam shook his head in irritation, then fixed his eyes on Noah. "You're killing me with this."

Noah kept silent as he waited for a response.

Sam finally gave in. "Fifteen minutes—that's it."

Noah nodded. He walked across the fort and took a seat beside Sam at the window. As he did, a particularly portly prairie dog yipped twice, bounded across the wooden floor, and launched into Noah's lap. P-Dog.

Noah petted his animal friend and asked, "How'd they get up here?"

Sam pointed to where a spiral staircase met a hole in the floor. The steps wound around the tree trunk. "And they used the same tunnels the tarsiers use. There's an opening under your shed."

"How long has it been there?"

"Probably longer than you've been alive."

Noah glanced at his shed and considered this. Then he scanned the tree fort. The prairie dogs were everywhere, getting into everything, their jittery movements making them seem frenzied. A small one stared into the eyepiece of Noah's binoculars and jumped back when the magnified images filled his vision. Another one had tunneled into a few *Star Wars* blankets that the scouts kept in the fort and was now lost in their folds, yipping in frustration. Another was probing through a pile of Richie's nerd-gear: shiny pens, tiny tools, and little electrical gadgets that blinked and bleeped and probably stored more data than all the computers at Clarksville Elementary.

"Seen anything weird?" Noah asked.

"You mean other than a kid running around his yard at night in his pajamas?"

Noah was about to ask who he'd seen, then became thankful that he'd figured it out before the question had left his lips. He nodded.

"Nope." Sam pointed out the window to the three rope bridges that connected the fort to lookout platforms on distant trees. "Are we certain the bridges can't be seen from the houses?" Sam asked.

Noah nodded. "Way too dark. Plus the trees and everything."

"Good. I'm going to post some of the prairie dogs on them. It can't hurt to put them to work. You cool with that?"

Noah nodded.

Sam said, "P-Dog . . ."

The prairie dog turned to Sam, who motioned to the bridges. P-Dog jumped off Noah's lap and, yipping softly, swept twice around the fort and then led six of his companions through the open doorway.

Noah watched in awe. "It still amazes me. The animals—the way they understand."

"Yeah, well, the communication only goes one way, let me assure you. To me, a growl is a growl, a grunt is a grunt, and a bark is as meaningless as a burp. They're sounds—nothing more."

"Can anyone understand them?"

"Some of the old-timers, yeah. Mr. Darby, a little. But with him just about anything's possible."

Noah nodded. A part of him already knew this.

Noah turned and stared silently into the night. For a bit, he watched the silhouettes of the prairie dogs move up and down the bridges.

"Who is he?" Noah's question came out of the blue.

"Who is who?"

"Mr. Darby."

Sam smiled. "He's the man. *Numero uno.*"

"Did he know Mr. Jackson, the guy who created the Secret Zoo?"

"I don't know. He doesn't talk about it, and nobody asks. Some say . . ." His voice trailed off.

"Some say what?"

"Never mind."

Noah thought to press the issue and decided against it.

After a few minutes, P-Dog scurried back to Fort Scout, his small silhouette just visible against the lighter shadows. He stopped at the window beside Noah, where he stood on his haunches and yipped once. Realizing that he wanted to be placed on the window frame, Noah scooped up his limp, trusting body and set him there.

For the next few minutes, Sam and Noah didn't speak. On the bridges, the prairie dogs continued to scamper back and forth, staring out at the yard. A few of them seemed to have given up and were now lying down, curled into the warmth and comfort of their own bodies, perfectly still and probably asleep.

Noah grabbed the scouts' binoculars and surveyed the zoo landscape. When he spotted the Knickknack and Snack Shack, his concern peaked.

"Do you think the sasquatches will try to escape?" he asked.

Sam nodded. "They're trying to get to DeGraff."

Noah felt his heart drop. "How do they even know who he is?"

For what seemed a long time, Sam said nothing. On the ground, the wind swirled the dusting of snow and rustled the dead, dry leaves. On the window frame, P-Dog sat on his haunches, his front legs dangling down over his belly.

Finally, Sam fixed his stare on Noah. "Why do you want to know this stuff, kid? It's only going to get you more involved. You still have a chance to stay out. The burden we're asked to carry . . . it's heavy. Too heavy."

Noah said, "Then share the weight."

Sam considered this. P-Dog stood at full height on the window frame, his dark eyes fixed on the Descender.

"You need to understand something right away," Sam said. "There's a connection between DeGraff and the sasquatches."

Noah's stomach dropped. Up to this point, the scouts hadn't considered the possibility of a relationship between the Shadowist and the sasquatches.

Sam brushed his sloppy bangs out of his eyes. Then he began to talk.

❧ CHAPTER 10 ❧

THE SECRETS OF THE SHADOWIST

"**I**'m guessing you've heard the story of how the Secret Zoo was built," Sam said.

Noah nodded. "Most of it, I think."

"Let me see if I can fill in any blanks." Sam settled into a more comfortable spot on the floor. "The story of the Secret Zoo . . . I guess it starts about a hundred years ago with Mr. Jackson, a rich guy from Clarksville. His wife died young, leaving him to care for their only child, Frederick. When Frederick was about twelve, Mr. Jackson adopted a monkey as a gift for him. Since they couldn't keep it indoors, they built a cage for it outside.

"In Clarksville, the monkey became a kind of celebrity. People were always gathered outside the Jackson mansion to see it. A rumor began that Mr. Jackson was adopting animals— exotic animals that owners realized they couldn't care for. The rumor jumped towns, cities, then states. More people started showing up. They brought a peacock, a crocodile, a bear, all kinds of weird things. They wanted Mr. Jackson to take their animals. And he did—he did because of how happy they made Frederick. For each new animal, the old man built a cage in his yard."

Noah said, "Then Frederick ended up dying, right? Unexpectedly, in his sleep. He died, and it was too much for Mr. Jackson to take, after losing his wife already. Mr. Jackson went crazy."

Sam nodded. He turned back to the window, hoisted the binoculars, and focused on something in the distance as he continued. "After Frederick died, Mr. Jackson couldn't stand seeing the animals in cages—not with the way they reminded him of his son. And the animals were too domesticated to return to the wild—doing that would have killed them.

"Out of nowhere, DeGraff showed up at Mr. Jackson's door, rambling about some guy from India, a person who could use magic to help Mr. Jackson build a massive underground zoo, a secret zoo, a place where Mr.

Jackson could release the animals. Bhanu. Mr. Jackson found Bhanu and asked him to come to America to build this place. Bhanu accepted, but on one condition. Bhanu was one of us, a member of the Secret Society, and what he wanted in return for helping Mr. Jackson was to use this world as a shelter, a safe haven for all the groups of the Secret Society, which were scattered across the world to protect different animals. Mr. Jackson accepted the terms, and the Secret Zoo was created.

"Around ten years later, the dwindling number of sasquatches in the Outside became a big concern for the Secret Society, and they launched an expedition to find as many as possible. By this time, Mr. Jackson was a full member of the Secret Society, and he spent a ton of money to send people all over the earth. They found about thirty sasquatches and moved them to the safety of the Secret Zoo. But once inside the City of Species, the sasquatches went wild and escaped into different sectors, where they went into hiding."

Noah nodded quickly, making the earflaps on his cap jump. The movement attracted P-Dog, who leaned over from the window ledge to give them a curious sniff.

Sam continued. "During this time, DeGraff somehow found his way into the Secret Zoo. We now know that he was the fourth brother. And being so close to Bhanu, Kavi, and Vishal, he came alive with magic—a magic he used to draw darkness into himself. Then he disappeared inside our borders for six months.

"With DeGraff so close, Bhanu and his brothers became more powerful. The Secret Arctic Town—you've been there, right?"

Noah nodded.

"Bhanu and his brothers created that entire sector in a single day. And the Forest of Flight—you've seen that?"

Again, Noah nodded.

"Two days. The whole thing. The Secret Society was in awe."

Sam lifted his binoculars and scanned the landscape again. Noah sat in silence and tried to connect the pieces of the story. After a minute or so, the Descender lowered the binoculars and picked up where he'd left off.

"The brothers' moods changed while DeGraff was inside the Secret Zoo. They started getting sick a lot. Headaches, fevers, nausea. No one understood what was going on.

"Their condition began to influence their creations. Especially in one sector, the Secret Creepy Critters. That place . . . it's dangerous. Some say it's filled with dark magic—*DeGraff's* magic. The animals inside . . . they're totally unpredictable. Some think the magic has changed them. They feed off each other, like in the Outside, and some kill for pleasure. These days we basically keep the sector off-limits to people—one of the Forbidden Five. Its gateway into the City of Species is constantly guarded, and we only allow animals that live inside the sector to pass back and forth."

"Why let the animals into the city at all?" asked Noah. "Why not just block off the entire sector, like the Dark Lands?"

"Too many people hope to rehabilitate the animals that live there. Some believe the goodness and light from the City of Species will burn away the darkness in their hearts."

Noah thought about this while Sam checked the landscape.

"The brothers got worse, and so did their moods. One day, things got crazy. For some reason they had a fight. And if the history of that day is even close to correct, you don't want to be anywhere near three magical guys when they're brawling. They destroyed entire sectors, and they just about killed each other."

"Why didn't the Secret Society stop them from growing the Secret Zoo?"

"They tried. But the brothers refused. And they were too powerful to stop. The Society could only stand back and hope for the best."

"Which obviously happened," said Noah.

Sam nodded. "A few weeks after their fight, the person

now known to be DeGraff was discovered and chased out of the Secret Zoo. The moment he was gone, the brothers returned to normal. The link was completely obvious, though at the time no one understood it. It took years of research to realize that the man who'd breached the borders of the Secret Zoo had been DeGraff. We learned that the circumstances of his birth were identical to those of his brothers, except that DeGraff was born in America, a world away from India."

Noah could barely believe what he was hearing. "And all that time, DeGraff was hiding in the Secret Zoo."

"Close," said Sam, "but not exactly right. DeGraff wasn't hiding—he was hunting."

"Hunting? For what?"

"For the first minions in his army."

"What—" Noah stopped himself. Though he was confused about many things, he understood where this was headed. "The sasquatches," he said. "DeGraff spent the six months that he was in the Secret Zoo assembling them."

Sam nodded. "That's the point I've been getting to." His face hardened, and his mouth twisted into a frown. "The sasquatches and DeGraff—they're on the same team."

❧ CHAPTER 11 ❧

THE SHADOWS OF DEGRAFF

"How . . . how do you know all this?" Noah asked at last.

The wind hissed and howled through the crevices of Fort Scout. Outside, a few snowflakes swept across the sky. On the window frame, P-Dog stood on his haunches, his stare shifting between Noah and Sam.

Sam leaned in close to Noah. "Get this. One night in the Secret Zoo, two doctors, a man and a woman, were working late. Sometime after midnight, they went for a walk. The entire City of Species was asleep—lights were out, and the city gateways were at a standstill. The sky was cloudless and crowded with stars. At some point, the doctors strolled into Sector Eighteen, a sector for lions, and guess who they came across."

"DeGraff?"

Sam nodded. "They couldn't see much of him in the darkness—just the circular brim of his hat and the long folds of his trench coat. He was standing just outside a cave, his back to the bright moon, his arms reaching out to the sky. At his feet, an enormous animal lay covered in his shadow. A sasquatch, either sleeping or dead.

"The doctors ducked behind some bushes and watched. DeGraff continued to stand with his arms raised to the stars, his fingers splayed. A minute passed. Then another. The sasquatch began to move. It rolled away, but DeGraff followed it, his arms still lifted, the moonlight still at his back. His shadow continued to blanket the sasquatch.

"The sasquatch went into a spasm, kicking and punching at nothing. For a moment, it became perfectly still. Then it hoisted itself to its feet, rising high above DeGraff to stare down on him."

Sam paused, leaving Noah to explore the image on his own. In his mind's eye, Noah saw the sasquatch towering above the Shadowist, moonlight glinting on its fangs. He saw its chest heaving up and down in greedy, shallow gasps. He saw its stare locked on DeGraff.

Sam continued. "Then the sasquatch simply turned

away and entered the cave. Just like that. There was no confrontation, no communication, nothing. The sasquatch just left.

"That was when one of the doctors moved, snapping a branch. DeGraff jerked at the sound, spotted them in the bushes, then fled across Sector Eighteen, disappearing within seconds."

Noah peered out at his dark neighborhood. Now everything about it was creepy: the trees, the peaks of shadowy rooftops, the spaces beneath backyard decks, the sheds and winterized pools. DeGraff could be anywhere, hiding in anything. How could they possibly stop him from getting inside the Secret Zoo? A place with a thousand points of entry—how could that be guarded?

Noah shivered, but not from the cold.

Sam continued. "The doctors ran into the City of Species and went straight to Security. Security sent hundreds of police-monkeys into Sector Eighteen and alerted the guards on the Outside. A guard in the Clarksville Zoo spotted him. And get this—the guard said that whenever DeGraff moved into a shadow, a deep one, he immediately appeared on its opposite side. It was like he could portal across them."

"That's . . ." Noah thought about it. "That's impossible." Then he remembered what Ella had said about the man she'd seen standing in the shadows of Richie's house on the night they first discovered the Secret Zoo. She'd said that he had dissolved into the shadows.

"Once on the Outside, it took only seconds for DeGraff to escape the Clarksville Zoo. Like this"—Sam snapped his fingers—"he was gone."

Noah waited to comprehend what had been said. "What about the sasquatch?" he asked at last. "What happened to it?"

Sam pulled his stare away from Noah. "It *became*."

When Noah realized that Sam wasn't going to add anything else, he prompted. "It became *what*?"

Sam looked at Noah again. In a heavy voice, he said, "Something else. Something . . . *different*. Somehow DeGraff's shadow . . . the magic inside it . . . somehow it poisoned the sasquatch."

Noah didn't like where this was going. He stayed silent and waited for Sam to go on.

"Shortly after DeGraff escaped, police-monkeys captured the sasquatch in the caves of Sector Eighteen. They locked it up in the City of Species. Right away, everyone could tell something was wrong with it. It was stronger and angrier than any sasquatch the Society had ever seen. And there was something in its eyes. An emptiness . . . or a deadness, maybe.

"The Secret Society built a containment area inside Sector Thirty-seven that became known as

CA-Thirty-seven. It was a large area, the size of a park, maybe, with thick perimeter walls. Over the next year, the sasquatch continued to change. It became taller, wider, stronger. Its hair grew long and fell out in patches. It sprouted fangs and claws. It was constantly in a rage and killed anything it could find—birds, snakes, bugs, whatever. It slept in the mud, tossing and turning and kicking its feet, no doubt plagued by nightmares.

"Incredibly, the world around it began to change. CA-Thirty-seven started to die. Grass wilted, waters muddied, and trees dropped their leaves. Somehow, just by its existence, the sasquatch was murdering the land. I know it sounds crazy, but DeGraff . . . it was like he was spreading his darkness through the sasquatch. DeGraff's wickedness . . . it's like a disease.

"In the end, the sasquatch became a monster—a *real* monster with full allegiance to DeGraff. And DeGraff didn't just get to that one sasquatch. In the months that he was inside our borders, he got to them all. And for DeGraff, that's only the beginning. He doesn't only want control over the sasquatches—he wants control over *all* the animals in the Secret Zoo."

Noah shuddered at the thought.

"Think of how the sasquatches have changed, and imagine what the other animals would be like. Think of a lion, a rhinoceros, an elephant. They'd become monsters of unimaginable strength. Think of what millions could do. Not just to our world . . . but to yours."

Noah did imagine it. And the ideas and images that formed in his head were terrifying.

Sam said, "This has been his plan from the very beginning—from the moment he stood on Mr. Jackson's porch telling stories of Bhanu. DeGraff wants an army of monsters to storm the earth."

Noah could feel his heart racing. Some things were beginning to make sense: Mr. Darby's stories; the Secret Society's concern about opening the Dark Lands to rescue Megan; the talk of the entire world being in jeopardy; and the urgent need to keep DeGraff out of the Secret Zoo. How could this be real? How could this be happening?

Noah suddenly felt very much alone. He scooped P-Dog up from the window and cradled him in his lap. P-Dog tipped his head to one side, then the other, his nose twitching. He stood on his haunches, sniffed at Noah's chin, then touched Noah's chest with a paw. The remarkable animal seemed to understand Noah's hurt—seemed, in fact, to want to share it, so that Noah wouldn't have to bear it alone.

Sam said, "I don't want to talk about this anymore. This stuff upsets me, and you need to get back inside."

Realizing Sam was right, Noah put down P-Dog and

went to the ladder. He took a few steps down and stopped. "What happened to the sasquatch in CA-Thirty-seven?"

Sam directed his stare to a meaningless spot in the yard and became very still. While searching for an answer, he seemed to have stumbled across a memory, and now he was wandering there. Noah would have given anything to see what Sam was seeing—to live as Sam in a part of his history.

"Sam?"

Noah's voice pulled the Descender back to reality. "Yeah?"

"The sasquatch . . . the one in CA-Thirty-seven. What did you guys do to it?"

Without another thought, Sam said, "We killed it. Just like we're going to kill every last one of them."

In the deep shadows of Fort Scout, Sam suddenly looked sinister: his eyes hidden in his bangs, his torso cloaked in his leather jacket.

"Go inside," the Descender commanded. "Go to bed."

This time, Noah obeyed without question. He fled down the ladder as fast as he could.

CHAPTER 12

DAMAGE IN THE PYTHON PIT

"**R**ight here," Tank said.

Tapping his fingertip on an impression in the ground, Tank was crouched low, his knees bulging out like boulders. The scouts were crowded around him, Richie peering over his shoulder and leaning against his mountainous frame. It was Wednesday, just two days after Noah's unnerving conversation with Sam in the tree fort, and the scouts were crosstraining with Tank in the Grottoes again.

"See the toes?" Tank swept his finger over five adjacent holes. He then traced his finger along a long arch in the imprint. "Sasquatch track. And it's fresh."

"You sure?" Richie asked.

The big man nodded, then lifted his head to stare down a dimly lit tunnel with brick walls and a dirt floor. A few other footprints were visible. They continued straight, then rounded a bend near a dusty velvet curtain. Tank stood, his bald head nearly touching the ceiling, and began to take slow, cautious steps down the passage, his arm waving behind him for the scouts to follow.

"Okay," Richie said in a hushed voice. "I think this is the part where I have a heart attack."

Ella whispered, "I'm with Richie this time."

In front of his friends, Noah followed Tank, occasionally craning his neck to peer around the big man's body. When Noah's foot dropped down a few extra inches, he lowered his gaze to see that he'd stepped into another sasquatch track. The impression was large enough to set a watermelon into. He swallowed back his fear and continued on, his heart hammering in his chest. As the five of them rounded the bend, he noticed the engraving over the curtain: "Platypus Playground." The tracks didn't go that way.

The Crossers continued another twenty feet down the dim passage and then stopped where the sasquatch had, a gateway marked "The Python Pit." Everyone knew the Python Pit was part of a greater exhibit called Snakes-A-Lot, which was completely independent from Creepy Critters, another building that housed snakes. The Python

Pit was a large inground exhibit full of trees and streams, and visitors stared into it from above. The sasquatch prints went beneath the curtain, then came back out.

"It went in and turned back," Megan said. "Why?"

Tank shook his head. "Don't know. But let's check it out. Who wants to go?"

Ella said, "I nominate you."

"And I nominate the smallest one of us," Tank said. "People tend to notice me—even when I'm not walking around in zoo exhibits."

"Then it's got to be Richie," Ella said. "He's built like a wafer. All he needs to do is stand sideways to disguise himself as a reed."

"Noah . . ." Tank said. "Go with him. Just stay back and keep your head up. When you cross into the Python Pit, it'll be into a cave in the fake mountainside in the middle of the exhibit. If anyone's around, just keep back to the cave." When both Noah and Richie hesitated, Tank said, "C'mon—you got to learn to do this stuff if you want to be Crossers."

Noah thought of the Descenders and the way they dismissed him and his friends as weak. Tank was right. If the scouts were going to make it as Crossers, they were going to need to do far more dangerous things than this. Without another thought, he grabbed Richie's arm, said, "C'mon," and stepped into the gateway.

As the curtain dropped down their backs, Noah and Richie appeared in the cave, just as Tank said they would. A slant of light fell through the mouth of the short cave and partially lit the floor and walls. Noah and Richie stepped aside to avoid the light and pressed their backs against the wall. With Noah in the lead, they slid down the wall and then stopped at the opening. Noah held his finger against the tip of his nose, an instruction for Richie to stay quiet. They listened. In the deep confines of the Python Pit, the splash of waterfalls was practically deafening. But there were no other sounds.

Noah slowly poked his head forward to stare out. About fifty feet away was the wall of the inground exhibit. It rose about twenty feet and then stopped at a railing on the tiled floor of Snakes-A-Lot. The wall ran in both directions and curved back behind the mountainside to complete a full circle. The Python Pit was crowded with small trees, small shrubs, and leafy vegetation. Vines fell from the heights, and a near-still stream eased along the grassy ground, its push provided by a distant waterfall. The moist air was fragrant with a backwoods smell.

Noah peered in both directions. He listened. No visitors seemed to be around. Just as he turned back to say something to his friend, the head of a python appeared by his feet. The snake slithered into the cave, revealing a bright green body flecked with white spots. It neared

Richie, circled his ankle, then coiled up his leg, its tongue flicking in and out. Richie clenched his jaw shut and nervously showed his teeth. When the python reached Richie's waist, it reversed direction, eased back to the ground, then slithered out of the cave.

"Oh . . . real nice," Richie said in a quivering voice. "Tell me—does the Grottoes have a portal to the bathroom? I think I peed my pants."

"Follow it," Noah said, his finger aimed at the python. "It wants to show us something."

"Why don't *you* follow it? I don't think—"

"Don't *think*!" Noah yelled in a whisper. "Just *do*!"

This jolted Richie into action. The skinny scout slipped past Noah and eased out of the cave, but not before uttering a few mild curses at no one in particular.

Noah peered out from the cave and watched Richie follow the python as it squirmed surprisingly fast through the tall grass and underbrush. With long strides, his friend tiptoed from one point to the next, the reflective material in his running shoes flashing in the overhead light. As his shoulders rocked, his hat's bushy pom-pom rolled in circles.

From the main floor of Snakes-A-Lot came a sound— the creak and groan of a swinging door. Then, through the noise of the waterfall, Noah could faintly make out footsteps. Someone was approaching. Noah watched as

Richie, who'd apparently heard the noise as well, splashed across the narrow stream. The python coiled up its long body and became perfectly still. When Richie was ten feet from the perimeter wall, he ducked a low tree branch, and a twig snagged his pom-pom and stripped off his hat. Voices erupted from above, and Richie, unable to reach back for his hat, turned and threw his back against the wall just as three young kids appeared at the rail directly above him.

In the shadows of the cave, Noah stared out with one eye. The children were laughing and pointing at different parts of the exhibit. One of them saw the green python and, with a wagging fingertip, revealed it to his friends. Some twenty feet beneath the children, Richie waited, his eyes wide with fear, his arms stretched out and his palms pressed against the wall. Ten feet away from him, his hat dangled. Big and bright, it was as out of place as a red tulip in a green pasture. It took only seconds for the children to notice it.

"Look!" one of the kids said, his voice rising above the sound of the waterfall. "Some *dork* dropped his hat!"

The kids laughed and pointed and clapped their hands. After a few seconds, they stared into the reaches of the exhibit, found nothing of interest, and darted off, their excited voices echoing off the hard walls of Snakes-A-Lot. The door squealed open and clattered shut again.

Noah waited a few seconds and poked his head out to see that Richie hadn't moved. With his back pressed to the wall and his face ripe with fear, he looked like someone standing on the ledge of a tall building. His hair, free from his hat, stood up in swirls and messy clumps. Noah waved his hand toward himself, a gesture that it was safe to continue, and Richie pushed off the wall, grabbed back his hat, and chased after the python, which had uncoiled itself and headed out again. Within seconds, Richie was led around the far side of the fake mountainside, and he disappeared from Noah's view.

As Noah waited, he looked around for signs that the sasquatch had been here. He saw places where the grass had been flattened, presumably by a large foot. Broken twigs dangled by unbroken bark, and some shrubs were partly crushed. He spotted something yellow stretched across the branches of a bush and realized it was a python. By the way its head drooped down, Noah was certain it was dead. Had it attacked the sasquatch only to be killed and flung into the bush? Noah moved his gaze and saw a still tail poking out from the distant end of the stream. Had the sasquatch murdered this snake, too? Squashed it with its big feet and then kicked it aside?

Noah spotted movement from the corners of his eyes and turned to look. Richie was charging back toward the cave, his eyes wide, his arms swinging wildly at his sides. He bounded a bush and then brushed past Noah into the cover of the cave. Noah swung around, saying, "What is it?"

Richie straightened his glasses, which had slid down to the tip of his nose to be fogged up by his excited breaths. "On the other side . . . there's a place where the railing"— he pointed to the railing along the pit—"is bent real bad. The python showed me by climbing along a branch."

"So? Maybe some fatso stood on it or something."

Richie shook his head. "The wall is damaged right below the railing. It's cracked . . . and a few places are punched out. And there are tufts of hair lying in the grass. The sasquatch . . . it grabbed the railing and scaled the wall, but it didn't escape. I saw its tracks on the ground of the Python Pit."

Noah moved his stare to a dark spot of the cave to explore his thoughts. "It could have escaped and it didn't. Why not?"

"The same reason the sasquatch beneath the Knickknack and Snack Shack didn't. It's scouting the grounds . . . preparing for something."

Noah turned back to Richie and again saw his nervousness.

"C'mon," Noah said. "Let's go tell Tank."

Richie nodded, and the two of them rushed to the end of the short cave and pushed through the curtain back into the Grottoes, Noah wondering how their news would change things.

CHAPTER 13

WIDE WALT IN THE MONSTER DOME

The next day, the scouts forced themselves to go to school and tried their best to feign interest in their class work. But being part of a secret civilization responsible for the safety of the world was growing to be quite a distraction. It was hard to solve for x and memorize state capitals when you knew monsters were prowling around in underground tunnels, threatening your neighborhood.

At lunch, the friends ate at a private spot on a cafeteria bench and quietly discussed the Grottoes and the things they had seen there. Around them, students drank their chocolate milk, ignored their vegetables, and shouted at friends. Spills occurred every few minutes, and crumbs flew like shrapnel from grenades. After eating, the four of them headed outside for recess and hunted down another place to talk. They settled on the vacant space beneath the large dome climber toward the rear of the playground. More than eight feet tall, the old steel climber was affectionately called the Monster Dome. It lacked the appeal of modern play structures, which sprawled in all directions, connecting slides and bridges and platforms. The Monster Dome frequently went unused, except by upperel students to hide out from second graders.

Just a few minutes into their conversation, three kids approached: Wide Walter White and his two cronies, Dave and Doug. As they neared, their big, angry feet kicked through the wood chips, stirring dust.

"Oh great," Richie said. "This doesn't look good."

Noah glanced around. As usual, there wasn't a playground attendant in sight. The scouts were alone, and Walt was undoubtedly aware of this. For him, bullying was a science.

The scouts hadn't confronted Wide Walt since their most recent altercation with the broad-shouldered thug. Just weeks ago, Noah had shocked Clarksville Elementary by tripping Walt in the cafeteria, nearly dropping him to the ground.

"Well, well," Walt growled as he approached. "The

Action Dorks, all together . . . and all alone."

Walt and his friends slipped through separate openings in the bars and stood just beneath the curved peak of the dome. The scouts jumped to their feet and nervously faced the schoolyard bullies. As Noah took a step forward, Megan lightly coiled her fingers around his wrist, holding him back.

Walt smiled at this. He crossed his arms over his chest, resting his forearms on the bulge of his gut. His shoulders were so wide that his head seemed puny in comparison. "Little sis going to fight your battles now?"

Walt's buddies erupted in exaggerated laughter. The chill air carried the fog of their breath, a stench of corn chips and cheddar cheese.

Walt grumbled, "We got some unfinished business, *dork.*"

Noah shook his head. "I don't have any business," he said. "Not with you." He discreetly scanned the playground in search of an adult. Behind Walt, a few kids had noticed the unfolding scene and were now busily alerting their friends, who began leaping off rock walls and throwing themselves from swings. Within a minute, they'd have the Monster Dome surrounded.

"I think you do," Walt said. And he reached up with one arm and shoved Noah. Hard.

Streaks of pain shot across Noah's chest and curled

over his shoulders. He struggled for balance and stood his ground.

Kids were already crowding the scene. Some were hollering. A young girl started to cry and ran off. Inside the open space of the dome, Noah suddenly felt like a fighter before a crowd of spectators—a wary gladiator in the pit of the Colosseum.

"Keep cool," Megan said.

Noah refused to turn his gaze from Walt. "Why do you want to do this? You ever stop to think that you create a lot of problems for yourself?"

"Oh, I create a lot of problems," Walt agreed. "But not for me—for other people." He held his open palms out to his sides in a what-do-you-think-about-that? fashion and glanced over at his buddies, a smug look on his face. "Whoever said I'm not a generous guy."

Grunting, Dave and Doug nodded their approval. Noah realized how small and insignificant they appeared beside their leader. Without Walt, Dave and Doug would be nothing—stardust in the galaxy of Clarksville Elementary.

"I got something I want to share with you," Walt said.

"What?" Noah said before he had time to think better.

"This."

Walt thrust his arms forward and pushed Noah again, harder than before. This time the pain shot all through his torso. He stumbled backward, toppled, and barely prevented himself from falling.

Ella jumped forward and shoved Walt, who barely budged. Walt turned to her and let out a disbelieving chuckle.

Ella propped her hands on her hips and pushed her elbows out to her sides. "Keep laughing, fat boy. I'll kick your—"

"White!" A voice rang out.

The crowd parted, revealing Mr. Kershen, the toughest sixth-grade teacher in all of Clarksville. He had a broad back, a shaggy mustache, and crooked yellow teeth. In another life, he might have been a Viking.

"White!" Mr. Kershen repeated. "You have *got* to be kidding me!" Everyone assumed that Wide Walt was the aggressor in any altercation.

Walt spun around and tried to looked surprised that something was wrong. "What?"

"Don't *what* me, Walter!" Mr. Kershen jerked his thumb toward the school. "To the principal's office. *Now.*"

Wide Walt slouched his gargantuan shoulders and kicked at the wood chips. He squirmed and squeezed his oversized body through a triangular opening in the dome climber and headed toward the school.

Mr. Kershen turned to watch the bully go. Then he faced the crowd of students and waved them away, saying,

"Get! Go do something, for crying out loud!"

As the children scattered, the scouts climbed out of the dome, Richie breathing a loud sigh of relief. Mr. Kershen stepped up to them.

"You guys okay?"

All at once, the four of them answered yes.

The rough-looking teacher looked them over. "That clown's bad news," he said at last. "Try to stay away from him."

"We do," Noah said. "All the time."

Wrinkles moved across Mr. Kershen's face as he formed a concerned expression. He nodded, knowing Wide Walt and knowing what Noah had said was true.

The scouts turned and headed for a new spot. Once again, they'd narrowly avoided a beating from the school bully.

Noah wondered how long they could continue to be so lucky.

❧ CHAPTER 14 ❧

BACK INTO THE GROTTOES

Later that day, their thoughts still on the incident with Wide Walt, the scouts reported to the Clarksville Zoo for crosstraining. They met Tank outside the Forest of Flight, where the big man stood with his arms crossed, his head gleaming. Tank turned and led them into the building. Inside, the air was thick with the earthy fragrance of grass, soil, and tree bark. A giant glass dome seemed to hover above a space filled with leafy branches and free-flying birds. The Forest of Flight was like a tiny jungle.

As Tank led the scouts down the visitor path, Richie

said, "Shouldn't the exhibit be closed for this?"

"Nope," Tank said. "You got to learn how to do this in the middle of the day."

They followed the path to a clearing where a family of four was staring up into the trees. They stopped along a rail and stared out, pretending to be interested in a rainbow-colored macaw perched on a branch. Noah realized how Tank loomed over Richie like a giant, his dark skin in stark contrast to Richie's pale color.

"Are we supposed to be keeping a low profile?" Noah whispered. "Because you guys aren't looking too much like father and son."

Tank chuckled and clapped Richie on his back, sending his pom-pom into a dance. Richie bumped against the rail and then reached up to correct his glasses.

After a few minutes, the family walked off around a corner and soon left the building. Tank glanced over his shoulders to make certain no one else was around.

A loud voice suddenly came from in front of them: *"Bwwwaccck! Tank! Secret Zoo! Bwwwaccck!"*

It had been the macaw. Now it was staring down at the Crossers, repeatedly tipping its head in new ways.

"You nuts, bird?" Tank said.

The macaw turned away and stared off into the distance, seeming slightly ashamed.

Shaking his head, Tank pointed into the exhibit. "See

that tree? There's a big hollow in the trunk on the other side. It goes down to the Grottoes. All you got to do is run out there and climb into it as fast as you can."

"But what about the other people?" Richie asked.

Tank looked around. "What other people?"

"There's no one here right now, but someone could walk in at any minute."

"Just be quick and you won't have nothing to worry about."

"But—"

"Megan," Tank said. "Show my boy Richie how it's done."

Megan smiled at the invitation and quickly slipped through the railing. She ran forward, startling birds into the air. Seconds later, she ducked behind the tree and was gone.

"See that?" Tank said. "Nothing to it."

"Maybe not for Megan," Richie said. "But she's like . . . like an empress of adventure. Me? I sort of trip on air."

Tank gently pulled down on Richie's shoulder, directing him between the rails. "Well . . . just make sure you trip into the right hole then."

Richie squirmed through the steel bars and then tore across the exhibit, the bright decals on his running shoes twinkling. He lost his balance, staggered a few feet, then ducked behind the tree and was gone. Ella went next.

To Noah, Tank said, "You're last, bub."

Noah shimmied through the railing and ran behind the tree. When he ducked into the hollow, he saw a dark passage dropping down about fifteen feet. A series of steps were built into one wall. He took them and landed in an adjoining tunnel with stone walls and an arched ceiling. The Grottoes. Tank fell in behind him, and the group gathered together.

"That was too easy," Ella said.

"It sometimes can be that way," Tank said.

Feathers of all sizes and colors surrounded their feet. Tank flattened them into the ground as he headed down the Grottoes, saying, "C'mon, gang."

The scouts chased after him. Birds swarmed from around a corner and flew up into the Forest of Flight. As Tank passed the portals, he called off their names: the Secret Metr-APE-olis; Koala Krossings; the Secret A-Lotta-Hippopotami. He led the scouts into a gateway marked "Grottoes WSE," and Noah felt the magic move through his body.

This new area of the Grottoes was much like the others. The difference was that the ceiling and walls were covered with small lizards. They were dotted and striped and patterned in ways that rivaled the designs in Richie's running shoes. Crawling all around, they created prismatic swirls of color. They were concentrated around a portal marked "A-maze-ing Geckos!," a Clarksville Zoo exhibit where visitors made their way through a maze with gecko-covered walls.

"Why aren't they in the Secret Zoo?" Megan asked.

Tank shrugged. "No idea. They like it down here for some reason. A lot of the animals do."

As the scouts moved forward, a few geckos jumped down to their shoulders and crawled along their backs. One landed in Megan's hair, looking a bit like a bright blue bow. Another one landed on Tank's bald head and clung to a spot just above his ear.

They crossed though a portal marked "Grottoes NNE" and walked past new gateways: "The Secret Cari-BOO!," "Little Dogs of the Prairie," "PizZOOria." Tank explained things as they went: when the gateways were built, why they were built, which ones were best to get to certain spots, which ones to avoid, which ones to plan on getting wet in, which ones might send you amiss. As they neared a gateway marked "A Fuss of Walrus," a broad, whiskered snout and two ivory tusks poked out from the curtain. Out came a walrus, clumsily walking on its flippers. Halfway into the Grottoes, it stopped, the curtain draped over its body like a bedsheet. As the scouts walked past it, they patted its blubbery side.

The scouts continued to explore for the next hour. They kept to the Grottoes and didn't venture into the exhibits or the sectors. Toward the end of their crosstraining, Tank stopped so suddenly beside a portal that Richie walked straight into his backside. The big man crouched low and picked up a matted tuft of hair. It matched the one they'd found near the Knickknack and Snack Shack.

"Sasquatch . . ." Noah said.

Tank nodded, his big, bald head rocking up and down. He stared at a spot on the ground, then ran his finger along a curved impression in the dirt. "See this?" he asked, his voice brought down to a whisper. "This is the heel."

The scouts squatted beside him. In front of the footprint was the indication of a second print. It showed how the sasquatch had walked through a nearby gateway. From their crouched position, the curtain seemed to loom above them, a velvet curtain on an ancient stage.

Noah felt a chill work across him. He suddenly realized how cold and quiet the tunnel was.

Tank said, "He went that way, that's for sure."

From the nearby curtain, something suddenly swung out—an arm with a mangy mess of hair. Curled claws sliced through the air, and a muscular hand seized Tank's arm. The big man was pulled off his feet and yanked through the portal.

Noah moved to go after him and stopped as the curtain was flung aside and two monstrous figures appeared.

Sasquatches. They snarled, saliva gooping over their lips.

Noah stepped back and stumbled over his friends, who were still crouched down. On all fours, he peered across the tunnel and spotted a gateway. He crawled to it, yelling, "GO! GO! GO!"

On their hands and knees, the scouts did.

A second before reaching the portal, Noah stared up to read the name of the place beyond it.

The Secret Polliwog Bog.

As the curtain stroked across his back, Noah realized the scouts had never been here.

❧ CHAPTER 15 ❧

THE SECRET POLLIWOG BOG

Just beyond the portal, Noah's palms pressed against something hard and flat and slick. Beneath him, the floor dropped a few inches and gave out in strange ways. Looking around, he realized that he'd crawled onto a stretch of lily pads across a dirty body of water—a bog or a swamp. The lily pads continued straight about fifty yards and stopped at a muddy shore. Not far into a wet, moss-covered woodlands, Noah saw a curtain dangling from a tree—the gateway into the City of Species.

Ella slammed against him and yelled, "MOVE! MOVE!" Noah sprang forward, almost like a frog, then took off crawling across the dense patch of lily pads. The floating leaves sank a few inches beneath his hands and knees, but were firm enough to keep him out of the water. His body dropped and shifted in odd, unexpected directions.

The lily pads were covered with frogs, green and brown and speckled. Hundreds sprang in all directions, their twiggy legs dangling beneath their bodies. They landed on Noah's back and struck his head like rubbery pellets fired from a toy gun. He peered back at the other scouts. Like him, they were struggling to crawl across the shifting lily pads, and like him, they were quickly being covered with frogs.

The curtain to the Grottoes flew to one side, and through the opening charged two sasquatches. Their weight was too much for the lily pads, though, and the monsters plunged in the water, leaving behind a series of circular waves. Noah stopped, and the other scouts turned back to see what he saw: the sasquatches were gone.

The four friends kept perfectly still and stared out. No one dared to speak. Around them, waves lapped at the lily pads, and frogs continued to hop. Fog hung in the air, and winged bugs buzzed by—dragonflies the size of hummingbirds. The distance played the *rum-rum-rum* sound of bullfrogs, constant and throaty.

A sasquatch rose in front of the curtain like a monster

on the stage of a horror show. It stood still, water dripping from its fangs. A few lily pads clung to it, their stems wrapped in its stringy hair. It snorted up water, then locked its eyes on the scouts.

It was blocking their way back to the Grottoes.

The water was up to the monster's chest, which meant it was over the scouts' heads. Noah looked out in all directions. Their best escape was into the City of Species through the portal on the shore.

"Guys . . ." Noah said.

Just then, the other sasquatch reached out from the water beside them and swung its arm down at Megan, barely missing her.

"Go!" Noah commanded.

He tried to stand, but his legs plunged though the lily pads. Crawling was the only way. The scouts moved as fast as they could, their arms and legs pitching wildly beneath them. Frogs continued to leap all around, their panic an echo of the scouts'.

About thirty yards from the shore, the sasquatch sprang up in front of Noah, who somersaulted onto his back and kicked the soles of his shoes into its chest. The beast splashed backward and became entangled in the long stems of the lily pads. Noah rolled onto his stomach and saw the now-distant portal back to the Grottoes. Just as Noah realized the other sasquatch was gone, a furry hand punched through the lily pads just behind his friends and swung through the air. The second sasquatch's claws barely missed Ella's head and sliced through a patch of frog-covered lily pads.

"We're cornered!" Richie hollered.

The sasquatch behind Noah untangled itself and slid back into the water. The scouts swung their heads around, trying to locate their monstrous adversaries in the murky bog. There was no sign of them.

"Which way?" Ella asked Noah. When he didn't respond, she barked, "Noah—which portal?"

"I . . ." Noah looked in front of them, behind them. He stared into the dark water over the ledge of the lily pads. "I don't know," he finally admitted.

"Keep still," Megan whispered. "If we can get both of them to one side, we can run to the portal in the other direction."

The scouts waited. No one moved. Or breathed. Even the frogs were still. Noah wondered how long the sasquatches could hold their breath.

Ella reached over into Richie's jacket.

"What—"

"Shhh!" Ella said. "Watch this."

When she withdrew her hand, she had Richie's penlight in it. She flicked on the switch and heaved it toward the portal to the Grottoes. It smacked down on the lily pads twenty feet away, its light clouded by a puddle of water.

"Get ready," Ella said.

The scouts braced themselves, suddenly conscious of what Ella was trying to do.

Both sasquatches sprang up at the same time beside Richie's penlight and swiped down at it, splashing water and ripping away lily pads. The scouts turned and crawled as fast as they could in the opposite direction.

"Go! Go! Go!" Ella screamed.

Noah's heart pounded. The lily pads continued to swing out in differing directions, their flimsy stems collapsing.

As the scouts closed to within twenty yards of the shore, Noah was suddenly hoisted into the air. Beneath him was a sasquatch. The beast shoved out its arms, and Noah flew through the air, his limbs flailing, then splashed down about forty feet away.

As Noah sank, the world went pitch-black and his winter clothes filled with weight. Unable to touch the pond floor, he swam to the surface, gasping for air. On the now-distant stretch of lily pads, his friends had stopped crawling and were staring out at him.

"Keep going!" Noah yelled.

He realized the water was churning. All around him, something was swimming; small, flexuous bodies squirming along his arms and legs. They felt like tiny snakes.

Between Noah and the lily pads, the sasquatch stood,

seaweed and muck clinging to its torso. It raised its arms, displayed the piercing points of its long claws, then roared and ran at him through the waist-deep water.

Noah turned to shore and swam, his arms swinging in wild arcs, his hands swatting through the things in the water. Waves spilled off his face and into his mouth. He understood nothing but to go—to go as fast as he could.

Something cinched his ankle and pulled him back. His nostrils burned as water was forced into them. Peering over his shoulder, Noah saw the sasquatch looming over him, its arm cocked. Just when he expected its claws to come down and tear into his body, the sasquatch abruptly released his leg and took a frenzied step away, its arms swiping through the water.

Noah peered into the dirty pond and realized what was happening. The tiny creatures were converging on the sasquatch. As hundreds streamed past Noah, he saw their dark, sinuous shapes.

The sasquatch rolled its head left and right and turned its body in fitful jerks. The water swirled and splashed as the curvy creatures moved in on it. They began to wriggle up through its mangy hair, rising out of the water along its arms and torso. Noah saw they were four inches long, with tails and bulbous heads. Tadpoles. He saw at least thirty, then forty, then many more. They squirmed up the sasquatch's arms and back and stomach. The confused beast swiped at its body, tearing out patches of fur. The tadpoles continued up its neck and over its head. Clutching its face, the sasquatch staggered to one side, lost its balance, then toppled into the water. The pond churned violently as a swell of tadpoles plunged after their prey, traces of moonlight gleaming on their slick bodies.

Noah didn't wait to see what was to become of the sasquatch. He turned and swam. A minute later, he pulled himself onto shore, muck oozing through his fingertips. As he scrambled to his feet, he saw the other scouts charging away from the lily pads. He merged into his friends, and together they headed for the gateway into the City of Species. Noah glanced around: there was no sign of the second sasquatch.

"Where is it?" Noah called.

"We don't know!" Ella answered.

The four of them dodged trees and hurtled through a web of exposed roots. They splashed through mossy puddles, ducked drooping vines, and plowed through patches of tall grass. Flying insects buzzed past, some pelting their cheeks and brows. Frogs of all sizes leaped out of the way. When they were twenty feet from the curtain, the second sasquatch jumped out of nowhere to cut them off. Hunched over, it growled, snarled, and spit.

The scouts stood braced to run in any direction.

Nearby, the tall grass shook and something big hopped out, startling them. Noah looked down to see a frog with a body bigger than a football and back legs almost as long as Noah's arms. Another frog of equal size sprang out of the marshy surroundings. Then another and another. Their giant bodies were slick and green.

"Richie!" Ella said. "What the heck are these things?"

"Goliath frogs, I think." Richie nervously jerked his head left and right. "Biggest frogs in the world."

Continuing to leap out, they crowded the space around Noah and his friends and then began to crawl onto one another, their dark, bulging eyes fixed forward. As the sasquatch lowered its head and peered around, drool spilled out from its scowl and plopped into a puddle. A frog jumped forward and landed near it. With a grunt, the monster lifted its big foot and tried to squash the frog, which sprang out of the way just in time. Mud and muck sprayed everywhere. When a second frog hopped forward, the sasquatch tried to kill it, too. A third frog advanced. Then a fourth, a fifth. In the air, their long legs dangled webbed feet as large and flat as flyswatters. One frog drove its snout against the monster's leg. Another struck its stomach. One jumped down from a low branch and pushed off the side of its head. The sasquatch swung its claws, missing the green aggressors while slicing through low-hanging vines.

As more and more frogs attacked, the sasquatch stepped back, blindly swinging its arms, batting an occasional frog out of the air. It got to within four feet of the portal, then three. Then it tripped over something and fell through the gateway, scores of goliath frogs pouncing after it. It was gone, and somewhere in the City of Species, it was still under attack.

"Un-be-liev-a-ble," Richie said as he watched the frogs launch themselves through the portal.

Noah took off running back the way they had come. "C'mon," he said. "We've got to find Tank."

Back at the pond, the scouts dropped down and crawled across the path of lily pads. As they went, Noah kept an eye out for the other sasquatch. There was no sign of it. Noah suspected the tadpoles—the weight of their unimaginable number—had drowned it.

At the end of the lily pads, they crawled through the portal and stood up in the Grottoes. Tank was there, bleeding from a cut above his eye and looking confused.

"Tank!" Megan cried out. "You okay?"

The big man nodded and forced a deep breath, his body shuddering. "You?" he managed to say.

They quickly exchanged stories. The scouts learned that Tank had fought off a sasquatch in the Secret Koala Kastle. When a group of koalas got involved, the sasquatch fled across the sector. They chased after it, but it managed to escape.

"I got to get back to the City of Species," Tank said. "Can you guys find your way out of here? Just go back to east-northeast and come out through Chinchillavilla."

The scouts nodded.

"Go as fast as you can. There might be others down here." He glanced around, seeming to consider something. "This is not good. The sasquatches . . . they're moving on the Grottoes, that's for sure." He struggled to catch his breath, then stared at the scouts. "They're coming for your world."

Richie gasped and took a step back. Noah felt his heart sink.

Without another word, Tank ran through the portal to Koala Kastle and was gone.

The scouts didn't hesitate. They hurried down the path that would leave the Grottoes and the increasingly dangerous world of the Secret Zoo behind.

CHAPTER 16

A Gift for Ella

More than a day passed without contact from the Secret Zoo. At school, the scouts tried to keep engaged in their routines, but elements of English and roles of Congress mattered none to them anymore. They did their best to avoid Wide Walt, which proved easy enough as teachers and parent volunteers were keeping a sharp eye on him after the Monster Dome incident.

On Thursday and Friday night, the Descenders continued their surveillance from Fort Scout. On both nights, Noah waited for his parents to fall asleep, tiptoed down to the kitchen, and peered out the window at the tree fort, a silhouette blurred by a sprawl of branches. Though he hoped to glimpse a Descender in action, he never did.

Now, the scouts were lounging in their fort. It was Saturday evening, almost eight o'clock, and the moon had long since replaced the early-to-tire December sun. The only light in Fort Scout came from the colorful Christmas bulbs strung around the place. Outside, a few snowflakes dotted the darkness. They painted the grass white, but amounted to no real accumulation. Richie sat at a table, probing the dissected organs of an electrical part. Noah lay in an oversized beanbag, tossing a tennis ball toward the ceiling again and again. Megan thumbed through one of her schoolbooks, and Ella stared out a window.

"It doesn't even feel like Christmas is coming," Ella complained.

"Well, there's the lack-of-snow factor," Richie pointed out. "But I'd guess it has more to do with the fact that sasquatches are trying to kill us. It's the kind of thing that can really put a damper on the holiday spirit."

Noah watched Ella leave the window and stroll across the fort. She stopped to press the button on a toy snowman sitting on a small table. Each of its three snowballs began to roll independently as a lousy hip-hop song professed he was a "Dancing Snowman! WOO! WOO! . . . Dancing Snowman! WOO! WOO!"

"I really want to punch this thing," Ella said.

"You're the one that bought it," Megan reminded her.

"I did?"

"Last year, remember? You said you loved it because it was just the right amount of 'perfectly annoying.'"

Ella pulled her eyebrows up. "Oh. Right." She watched the snowman shift its round rump in new directions. "How come now all I want to do is take its batteries out?"

When no one responded, she trudged over to the giant beanbag and plopped down beside Noah, almost catapulting him off it. As Noah gripped the beanbag, the falling tennis ball bounced off his head and rolled into a corner.

"And why haven't we heard from Marlo in so long?" Ella asked.

"It hasn't been *that* long," Noah answered. "Barely two days."

"Yeah, well . . . feels long to me. How am I supposed to get on with life with all this weirdness going on?"

"I know," Megan said. "Everything feels so . . . strange, like I'm living in a movie."

"A movie *in* a movie," Richie added.

Noah nodded. His old life seemed a distant memory, his old world a faraway place. His new world, the one that involved the Secret Zoo, was unlike anything he could have imagined.

"Do you think Tank's okay?" Megan asked. "I mean . . . he got cut pretty bad."

"Tank?" Richie said. "That guy could walk away from a nuclear bomb." He held an electrical piece toward his friends. "Hey, what do you guys know about reading the color band of a resistor?"

Ella said, "About as much as I know about building a satellite. Or milking a cow."

"Don't ask me," Megan said. "I don't do electronics."

Noah shrugged.

The scouts became quiet for a while. Christmas lights blinked on and off, casting shadows in new ways. Noah reached out his arm to reclaim his tennis ball. Megan read her book. Richie paddled his fingertips through his spill of circuitry. Ella rose, walked to the toy snowman, and pressed its button again. The snowman rolled and shimmied as his song played: "Dancing Snowman! WOO! WOO! . . . Dancing Snowman! WOO! WOO!" She turned it upside down and gutted its batteries.

When the scouts started up conversation again, the topic returned to the Secret Zoo. An hour blurred past as they discussed the Grottoes, the portals, the City of Species, and the sectors. They recalled their adventures in the Wotter Tower, the Secret Metr-APE-olis, the Dark Lands, and the Secret Polliwog Bog. They wondered about the Shadowist, Kavita, the Forbidden Five, and all the Descenders they had yet to meet. There was so much to the Secret Zoo—so much they didn't understand.

Would they ever? Noah hoped they would.

At some point Ella walked over to the small Christmas tree against one side of the fort. Less than two feet tall, the tree's sparse limbs held only a few dull ornaments, bulbs that had barely avoided being pitched away several years ago. The tree, dry and frail, seemed to be warning the world that it could topple at any moment.

"Honestly, Richie . . ." Ella said, knowing he had picked out the tree. "Did you swipe this thing from Charlie Brown, or what?"

"Show it your love and it'll show you its beauty," Richie said. "Just like anything else."

Ella touched one of its limbs, and needles rained off her fingertips. "Talk about a fire hazard." Four presents were tucked beneath the tree. Ella crouched and sifted through them, reading the tags. Then she stood straight, sighed, and again remarked, "It doesn't even feel like Christmas."

A strand of lights flashed, revealing Ella to Noah. Her lips were quivering, her eyes brimming with tears. She wasn't just being grumpy—she was truly sad. And as Noah abruptly realized why, his heart sank. Several years ago, Ella's parents had divorced. Her father moved away, and these days Ella almost never saw him. It didn't feel like Christmas to Ella not because there wasn't snow, but because it was the time of year for families, and her father was gone. With everything going on with the Secret Zoo,

Noah, Megan, and Richie had simply forgotten.

Noah sprang off the beanbag and rushed over to the tree. "Let's open the gifts!"

"Seriously?" Ella asked.

He scooped up his present. "Seriously."

"But we always wait until Christmas Eve," Ella said. "It's a tradition."

"What's the value of tradition without the threat of change, huh?" Noah playfully bumped Ella. "This holiday season, I propose we become that threat."

"Wow . . ." Ella said. She quickly wiped away a tear before it could fall. "Big words and bigger ideas. You sounded like Richie."

As Ella turned to the gifts, Noah peered around her back and mouthed, *Her dad* to Richie and Megan, who then jumped to their feet and rushed to a spot by the tree.

Ella said, "I've been so grouchy . . . I'm sorry, guys. I just miss . . . you know . . ." She swallowed back a whimper.

Megan draped her arm over Ella's shoulder and pulled her close. "We know," she said.

Ella became very quiet for a very long time. The scouts waited for her. Her chest fluttered as she swallowed back a cry, then she said, "Sometimes . . . sometimes I . . . never mind."

Megan rested the side of her head against Ella's. "It's okay, girlfriend."

Everyone became quiet and shared in Ella's pain. A few minutes passed. Different strands of light blinked on and off, rearranging the shadows. The wind whistled, and a distant car revved.

"Who wants to go first?" Megan asked.

Richie didn't hesitate, and wrapping paper flew through the air. An ultra-sized pack of batteries was quickly revealed.

"For your nerd-gear," Noah said with a wink.

"Thanks, man!"

Megan went next. Her gift was from Ella. She quickly unwrapped twenty-four glow-in-the-dark Silly Bandz shaped like zoo animals. "Way cool!"

Noah's gift was from Megan. A new watch.

"To replace the one you lost in the Secret Zoo," she explained, referring to the watch he had ruined in the cold waters of Penguin Palace during his first journey inside.

Noah smiled and slapped the watch across his wrist.

Richie shoved the last gift at Ella. "Here. From me."

Ella turned the box over in her hands. Her eyes had dried up, and she seemed herself again. "Oh, great. Richie drew my name this year. Can't wait to see what I got. A girl can never have too many penlights, you know."

The scouts chuckled together. Then Ella shredded the wrapping paper, reached into the box, and dangled the gift across her fingers. A charm bracelet. Silver with round links, it had five charms, each with one or more words on it.

"What do they say?" Megan asked.

Ella stayed quiet for what seemed a long time. Finally, she read them out loud. "Megan. Noah. Ella. Richie." She paused for a few seconds then read the last charm. "Best Friends Forever."

A flash of colorful light revealed the start of Ella's smile. She slipped her wrist into the bracelet, then held it in front of her. The blinking Christmas lights sparkled on the shiny silver. A fresh tear welled in her eye.

Richie said, "You have no idea how hard it was to find 'Noah' as a charm," as he stuffed batteries into his jacket pockets. His flat, casual tone suggested he had no idea that his gift had touched Ella's heart. "I think I spent a week Googling that thing. And then I had to pay a small fortune for shipping."

Ella's shoulders went limp. Her smile grew. "It's . . ." She raised her hand and allowed the bracelet to slide a bit down her arm. "It's really great, Richie."

Just then, Mrs. Nowicki called out for her children to head indoors.

"Coming!" Noah shouted. He quickly gathered up the wrapping paper, wadded it, then shot it into a wastebasket. "C'mon, guys," he said. "Time to go."

They stood, gathered their things, and headed to the slide. Megan went first. As Noah prepared to go, he glanced over his shoulder and spotted Ella hugging Richie. As they released each other, the lights flashed and Noah saw Ella's lips move in a soundless *Thank you*. Noah, sensing he was intruding on a private moment, turned and sped down the slide.

After a bit, Ella and Richie joined them on the ground. The friends tore across the backyard, leaving faint footprints in the dusting of snow. Richie and Ella headed to the street, and Megan went inside. At the door, Noah reached down and unplugged the extension cord for the lights. Fort Scout stood empty and dark.

For now.

But in just a couple of hours, it would be invaded again. This time by another set of visitors—very different visitors with very different intentions.

The door closed, leaving behind Noah's world like an offering to the night.

❧ CHAPTER 17 ❧

RICHIE GOES BLIND
AND CHOCOLATEY

"What time is it?" Ella asked Richie.

The two of them were walking home from Noah and Megan's, Richie's pockets full of new batteries, and a new charm bracelet dangling from Ella's wrist. They were expected by their parents to go to Ella's house, where a few neighborhood moms, including Richie's, were playing cards.

Richie pulled back his sleeve. "Almost nine-thirty."

Ella scanned the surrounding yards. "Which is a lot like almost ten o'clock."

"Huh?"

"The tarsiers, they come out at ten."

Richie glanced into the trees. "That's right. I almost forgot."

Ella stared into the bushes in Mrs. Johnson's yard. Then she peered into the hollow of a tree. "Don't you think it's weird that we've never seen them. I mean, *never*."

Richie shrugged. "You saw how small they are. And the way they blend with the trees."

They turned onto another street and neared Ella's house. As they headed up the driveway, Ella reached out and plucked away Richie's glasses.

"Hey!"

She stuffed them into her pocket. "I'm going to need these."

"What are you—"

"Let's check out the tarsiers! We'll tell our moms that you forgot your glasses at Noah's. That'll give us a reason to go back out. We can go into the woods by the Millers', just for a few minutes."

Richie considered this. "I don't know," he said at last. "What if—"

"Quit being such a wimp!"

As they turned onto the sidewalk leading to the front door, Richie felt his way, his hands probing the space in front of him. "I can't see a thing without my glasses!" His ankle slipped off the edge of the concrete, and he almost fell.

Ella grabbed his wrist and escorted him onto the porch. Richie stumbled on the welcome mat and banged his forehead on the door. Someone inside hollered, "Come in!" and Ella burst out laughing.

"You could always try the doorbell," Ella teased as she led Richie into the house.

A group of women were seated around the dining room table. They were sipping wine and holding spreads of playing cards that looked like Asian fans.

"Why, here they come now!" Richie's mother said. Her cheeks were flushed, and she seemed a bit cheery. "We were just wondering about you two! I was just about to call—" She stopped herself short and swung around in her chair. "Richie, where are your glasses?"

Richie squinted down at his mother. "Huh?"

"Your glasses. How come you're not wearing them?"

Richie groped at his face. "Oh great. I must have left them at Noah's."

Ella peered over at him. "I thought you looked weird. More than normal, I mean."

At Ella's joke, the ladies spasmed with laughter. Mrs. Morris set down her cards and squarely clapped her palms.

"Well, you'll have to go get them," Mrs. Reynolds said. "Right away."

Ella checked the clock and saw it was still more than

twenty minutes until ten. She had to stall.

"Let's get a cup of hot chocolate first." She went to the cupboard in the kitchen and pulled out two white packets. "We're freezing. It's snowing out there, you know."

"Is it?" the ladies said in various ways. They turned to the picture window and discovered the drapes drawn. None of them cared enough to get up and open them.

"Not much," Ella added. "Just enough to cover the grass."

"Well, thank goodness for that," Mrs. Cooper said. "It's too early to be shoveling the driveway."

The ladies turned back to their game, nodding and groaning in ways that expressed their agreement.

Ella filled two cups and placed them in the microwave. Richie eased into the kitchen, the tips of his flashy sneakers reflecting off the floorboards, the oven, the refrigerator. The microwave dinged, and Ella lifted the steamy cups. She set one on the countertop in front of Richie. "Very hot. Don't burn your face off."

Richie raised the chocolately drink to his lips, blew steam across the room, and took a sip. Chocolate spilled down his chin.

"Honestly, Richie." Ella swept up a nearby napkin and dabbed his chin like a mom. "How blind are you?"

Richie peered at her. "Let's just say your face looks like someone squashed it with a really big thumb."

The two of them slurped their hot chocolate and watched the clock. Minutes slipped by. In the dining room, the ladies shuffled cards and laughed too loudly. As soon as the clock read 10:00, Ella and Richie dumped their cups into the sink and headed down the foyer.

"We'll be back," Ella said as she opened the front door.

"Be careful!" Ella's mother called out. "Don't let the bogeyman get you!"

The two scouts shared a nervous look between them. Then they turned and walked out.

CHAPTER 18

CATCHING SNOWFLAKES

Ella and Richie hunkered down and headed across the Millers' backyard. The property backed against a wooded area between two sides of the neighborhood. In the thick of the trees, the scouts dodged trunks and fallen branches. They stopped in a clearing and stared out in different directions. A few houses were barely visible, their lights off. Confident they couldn't be seen, the scouts moved their attention to the treetops.

"I don't see any," Ella said.

"Me either," Richie said. He adjusted his glasses, which Ella had given back to him on their walk over.

Around them, a few snowflakes fell.

"Are they even out here?"

Richie shrugged. "Tameron said ten o'clock, right?"

She nodded. Hearing Tameron's name made her think of the Descenders. She wondered if they could see them from their zoo posts and decided there was no way.

They strolled around a bit, their gazes held toward the heights. The web of branches was perfectly still. Richie crouched beside a hollow of a trunk and shined his penlight in. He straightened up and shrugged his shoulders. Nothing.

"We need to go up," said Ella.

"Up where?"

Ella pointed into the heights. "There."

"I don't think—"

"C'mon! It'll just take a second. I want to see these little furbies. "

"You know how I climb."

Ella grabbed his wrist and pulled him over to a tree. She knelt and cupped her hands out in front of her—a step for Richie's foot. "Here. The first limb's always the toughest."

"And the second. And the third. And—"

"Richie!"

He mumbled something under his breath and then planted his foot in her hands. He pushed up and landed his other foot in the crook of a limb. As he tried to lift himself, he lost his balance and fell to one side, his rear end touching down on Ella's head.

"Gross!" Ella groaned. "Your butt is *totally* on me!"

Richie found his balance and climbed into the tree. As Ella stood straight, she scrunched up her face and shook out her hands. "Ew," she said. "Just *way, way* ew."

She hurried to the neighboring tree, jumped into it, and ascended with the grace of a gymnast, her movements long and sweeping and exact. Richie battled his way up, cinching branches and clutching the trunk. At about twenty feet, Ella stopped and waited for Richie. In quite a few minutes, he joined her in the heights.

"See anything?" Ella asked.

"Nuh-uh. But my eyes are closed."

Ella looked over and realized he was serious. *"Richie!"*

He forced his eyes open. Then he stared all around. "Nope, no tarsiers. I don't think they're even out here."

Ella considered this. It didn't make sense. This was probably the most wooded area in their neighborhood. Wouldn't the Secret Society want to pay close attention here?

A snowflake landed in her eye and blotted out the world. She wiped it away and peered up. The once-thin snowflakes were now plump. They fell from the sky like silvery coins. As they touched down on Ella, they briefly kept their shapes before melting away.

"It looks like—"

She cut herself short and listened. She'd heard some-thing. A soft squeak.

"What's wrong?" Richie asked. "Did you—"

Ella held up a pink glove, stopping him. Then she qui-etly slid over to a new branch, her ears perked up.

Eep! The noise again.

She ducked her head for a new angle and spotted some-thing along a vertical branch. Was it a bump? No. She swung her head around and saw a small, furry body with two upturned ears and round, bulging eyes. A tarsier. It was looking straight at her.

Eep!

Ella slowly moved to a new branch. "Hey, buddy."

The tarsier crawled to a spot just inches in front of Ella's nose. The critter was tiny—barely the size of a hamster. Being so close, Ella could make out its details. It had long, thin fingers with tips that looked like suction cups. Its rear, kangaroolike legs were tucked against the sides of its body.

Without warning, the tarsier sprang from the branch and landed on her shoulder, just beside her cheek. Then, as if from nowhere, a second one touched down on her other shoulder. The animals traded *eep!'s* and settled into stable positions, their fingers stuck to her jacket.

"You guys are way cool."

"Ella!" Richie called. "You see anything yet?"

"You could say that." She swung around the tree trunk

to show her discovery.

"Oh my gosh!" His eyes had swelled to twice their normal size. "You found them! Are they friendly?"

"Seem to be. You haven't seen any?"

"Nope. I think my tree's empty. I'm going back down."

As Richie started to descend, Ella saw that his back had three very peculiar bumps along it.

"Richie, you're covered in tarsiers!"

"Huh? What are you talking about?"

"Your back—you got three on it."

He became deathly still and seemed to consider this. "What should I do?"

"Not what you'd normally do, which is scream and fall from the tree. I don't care so much about you, but the tarsiers . . . they're kind of cute."

Richie glanced over his shoulders and tried to see down his back. "What are they doing?"

"It looks like they're getting ready to chew off your cheeks."

Richie's expression opened with fear.

Ella shook her head. "You dork. Meet me on the ground."

She climbed down and waited beneath Richie's tree. On her shoulders, the tarsiers craned their necks to watch the action. Richie successfully navigated to a new branch, then another. When he tried to go to a third, he slipped, almost fell, then released a mild profanity into the night.

The tarsiers turned to Ella, their bulbous eyes seeming ripe with concern.

"Don't worry," Ella advised. "He's actually doing pretty good. I thought he'd be dead by now."

Richie touched down to the ground and swung his back toward Ella. "What are they doing now?" he asked, concern blending his syllables.

"Sitting there. Looking cute." She reached out her arm, and a tarsier jumped to it like a parrot. She shoved the animal toward Richie. "Check him out."

"Last time I did that I almost had my head swallowed."

"Well, this one doesn't look hungry. Now, hold out your arm." When Richie did, Ella shook her arm a bit. "Go get him, Gizmo."

The tarsier kicked out its hind legs and hopped through the air like a frog. It touched down on Richie's forearm and shot its wild-eyed gaze up at him. It *eep*ed once. As Richie nervously looked it over, Ella reached behind him for another tarsier.

"It is sort of cute," Richie said. "If you can see beyond the terror of the experience, I mean."

Ella pitched her arm in front of Richie again. "Here," she said. "Have another."

The tarsier lunged onto the front of Richie's jacket, climbed into one of his pockets, and poked its head out. The two scouts started laughing, Richie a bit tensely.

"How funny!" Ella said. "He looks like—"

She stopped short as the tarsier on her left shoulder sprang several feet into air. It chomped down on a fat snowflake, then landed on her shoulder again, its eyes wider than ever from the shock of the cold.

As the scouts broke out laughing again, the tarsier on Richie's back leaped off, snagged a snowflake out of the air, and landed on Ella's arm.

"Too cool!" Ella said. She stepped into the clearing for a place where the snowflakes could have an unobstructed fall. She looked up and saw them streaming down from the night's nothingness. They were bigger than quarters. "Richie! Over here!"

In the clearing, Richie faced Ella, about ten steps dividing them. A tarsier kicked off Ella's arm and shot forward. It gulped a snowflake in mid-flight, then grabbed on to Richie's leg. The tarsier on Richie's shoulder went next. It soared through the air, its long legs dangling behind it, and caught a snowflake before landing on Ella, where another pushed off and flew across the distance back to Richie.

Ella said, "They're so strong!"

The strange little animals continued like that, one after another streaking through the open area between Ella and Richie. They pulled snowflakes out of the air and gobbled them down. Ella didn't know if they thought the icy crystals were bugs, or if they were just having fun. Maybe both. Or maybe they were just happy to be playing with the scouts.

A tarsier landed on Richie's head, plowed over his pom-pom, then fell down to his back. Ella went into a fit of laughter. Seconds later, another tarsier missed Ella and passed over her head. It grabbed onto a nearby branch and quickly sprang back, striking down on one side of Ella's fluffy earmuffs, knocking them askew.

A cloud emptied a fresh load of snowflakes. Big and white and patient, they floated down into the clearing, dotting out the scenery. To Ella, parts of Richie kept disappearing. Sounds softened. The crunch of leaves beneath Ella's feet, the *eep!'s* of the animals, Richie's laughter—the noises dulled as they passed through the filter of the falling snow.

Excited by all this, the tarsiers jumped back and forth with new energy. They ping-ponged off Ella and Richie, speeding past one another in the air. Each time one landed on Ella, she watched its big eyes blink away the snow. Snowflakes melted on their bodies and matted their fur.

Within minutes, the storm slowed down. And with it, so did the tarsiers. They settled on the scouts, three on Ella, and two on Richie. Ella felt their slight shudders as their tiny chests heaved.

"We better go," Ella said. "We should have been home a long time ago."

Richie nodded, and the two of them hurried over to a tree. The tarsiers climbed onto the branches and stayed perched in low spots. They suddenly seemed exhausted.

"Later, dudes," Ella said. Then she turned and led Richie out of the woods.

By the time they reached the street, the snow had already died down. Most of what was on the ground probably wouldn't survive the night. As they walked, Ella turned again to the treetops. Somewhere in them, hundreds of tarsiers were perched on branches, perfectly still and hidden. She imagined their bulging eyes staring down. Right now, they could see her and Richie. They even knew what the two of them had just done.

"We've been watched," Ella said. "Our whole lives. Every night."

"Yeah," Richie said. "And maybe not just by the tarsiers."

She turned to him. "What are you talking about?"

Richie lifted his eyebrows. "DeGraff."

With all their concern on the sasquatches lately, Ella had almost forgot about the Shadowist. She swept her stare across the nearby yards. Bushes, sheds, corners. Was he somewhere out there? Was he watching them right now?

Ella shuddered.

"C'mon, Richie. Let's get the heck out of here."

The two of them bolted up the street, away from the hiding spots in the yards, and beneath the watchful stares of the tarsiers.

❧ CHAPTER 19 ❧

ROGER, ROGER

When the final school bell rang on Monday, the scouts snatched their backpacks from their lockers and ran to the bathrooms, where they used the stalls to change into their zoo uniforms—ugly button-up shirts with vertical stripes and long, flat collars—that disguised them as zoo volunteers. Back at their lockers, they threw on their jackets and winter gear, then squirmed down the crowded halls and pushed through the exit, the cold air rushing into their lungs. They bolted across the playground, across the street, then through the west entrance of the zoo, which was adjacent to Clarksville Elementary.

At the entrance to Butterfly Nets, a familiar sign read "CLOSED FOR CONSTRUCTION!" Noah plucked the magic key from his pocket, checked over his shoulders, then cracked open the door, saying, "Voilà." The scouts turned their shoulders to slip inside.

They headed around a turn and were met by a sight that caused them to stop in their tracks. Just off the path, Tank was standing among the trees. He was surrounded by a group of animals—a polar bear, an emperor penguin, and no fewer than fifty prairie dogs, which were running around the feet of the other animals in a frenzy, stirring the fallen leaves. The scouts recognized the animals immediately as Blizzard, Podgy, and P-Dog and his pals. Also with Tank were the Descenders—Sam, Hannah, Tameron, and Solana. Solana wore her soft blue leather jacket and fingerless gloves—clothes that twelve-inch quills could spring from. Her long, smooth hair looped around her ears and dropped down her back. She was beautiful.

"Oh my gosh!" Megan said as she glanced over her shoulders in a nervous way. "What's everyone doing here?"

Ella was more direct in sharing her surprise: "Are you guys out of your minds?"

Tank reached out one of his meaty arms and scratched Blizzard behind the ear. "Don't sweat it—we aren't staying."

Ella said, "But what are—"

"After what happened last week, Mr. D and the Secret Council have made a change of plans."

"How so?" Noah asked. Marlo suddenly shot out of the treetops and took a spot on his shoulder, landing with a chirp.

Tank rubbed his jawline, saying, "We're going to beef up patrol in the Grottoes. The Gifteds—we're sending in some of them."

The scouts knew that the Gifteds were animals that had adapted in the Secret Zoo. They had greater awareness and communication skills, and some Secret Cityzens believed the magic of the Secret Zoo had changed them. The animals in front of them—Blizzard, Podgy, and P-Dog—all were Gifteds.

Blizzard rolled his snout and growled, and Podgy raised his flippers a bit.

"Where's Little Big?" Richie asked.

"He's waiting for us just inside the Grottoes. We tried to squeeze him up the staircase, but it didn't happen."

Blizzard growled, as if to acknowledge the struggle.

Noah turned to the Descenders and said, "What are you guys doing here?"

"Yeah," Ella said. "Don't you guys ever sleep?"

"Now and then," Solana replied.

Tameron said, "Lately a lot less 'now' and a lot more 'then.'"

Sam took a step toward the scouts. "We're going to show the Gifteds around the Grottoes today. And show you guys how to use these. . . ."

Sam nodded to Tank, who reached into his jacket pocket, pulled out a fistful of stuff, and one by one tossed something to each of the scouts. After Noah snatched his out of the air, he took a look at it. Noah could tell that the small plastic piece full of electronics was supposed to fit in his ear.

"A radio," Tank said. "The same kind me and the Descenders wear. You turn it on, plug it into your head, and let the technology of your world do its thing."

The mention of technology excited Richie, and he immediately set his in. "Sweet! How does it work?"

When Tank touched his ear, Noah realized the big man could now hear Richie's voice through his speaker. "Bone mics to talk. A switch controls voice activation, if that's your game. The signal's scrambled, so no one but us can hear." Tank moved his stare off the scouts and said, "Red, you there?"

Richie pulled his head to one side, as if surprised by what was surely Charlie Red's voice in his ear. "I hear him!" Richie said.

Tank nodded. "And he hears you."

As the other scouts plugged their headsets into their ears, Noah heard their voices.

Ella said, "But how can we hear one another when we don't have microphones?"

"We do," Richie said. "Bone mics work from bone conduction. When you talk, vibrations carry through your skull. Bone mics pick up those vibrations and translate them to your voice."

"Way cool!" Ella said. "Meg—can you hear me?"

"Roger," said Megan with a turn of her head. "How about me?"

"Roger, roger." Ella spoke in her best battle droid voice. She turned to Tank. "Can other people in the Secret Zoo hear us now?"

"Not a bit," Tank said. "The radio signals can't pass through the portals between the two worlds."

"So they only work in one world or the other?"

Tank nodded.

"Roger, roger." Ella joked again. She dropped her smile and turned a confused look to her friends. "By the way— why do radio people always say 'roger'?"

Richie said, "'Roger' used to be the phonetic designation for the letter R, which stands for 'received.'"

"Wow," Ella said. "So not only do I know that . . . but I also got to hear 'phonetic' in a sentence." She turned to Tank and said, "All this knowledge . . . if you hang with Richie long enough, you'll seriously feel your brain swell."

"Roger that," Richie said into the air—and his bone mic.

The scouts shared a quick laugh; then Tank said, "C'mon, let's go for a walk."

Noah led the way off the path and walked past Blizzard, saying, "C'mon, Bliz. Follow us."

The other Crossers—humans and animals—followed Tank across the wooded terrain, their paws and feet crunching fallen leaves and splashing through streams. They walked behind the large rock formation to where the familiar flight of stairs led to the Grottoes. Then, one by one, the Descenders, the scouts, the Gifteds, and Tank stepped into the magic system of tunnels beneath the Clarksville Zoo.

ᘓ CHAPTER 20 ᘔ

GIFTEDS IN THE GROTTOES

"**Y**ou guys see anything?" Noah asked into his bone mic, referring to sasquatch tracks. He was walking with Blizzard and Sam in the NSE end of the Grottoes. After entering the tunnels beneath Butterfly Nets, the Crossers had met up with Little Bighorn, and Tank had divided them into groups: Noah with Blizzard and Sam; Ella with Little Bighorn and Solana; Megan with Podgy and Hannah; and Richie with P-Dog, the prairie dogs, and Tameron. Then Tank had walked off to investigate on his own.

"Nuh-uh," said a girl's voice into his ear. Ella.

"Nothing here," said Megan

"Negative," said Richie.

"Just me and the walls," said a fifth voice that Noah recognized as Tank's.

As the airwaves fell silent, Noah concentrated on the tunnel around him. Lined with old bricks, the walls reached several feet over his head to support an arched ceiling. The dirt floor was pitted with shallow holes. A few fluorescent bulbs were set in the walls, and shadows pooled just beyond their dim throws of light. Occasional velvet curtains marked portals to new spots. Noah passed a gateway to Arctic Town, the Secret Rhinorama, and the south end of the Grottoes.

"Bliz," Noah said to the mighty polar bear beside him. "Remember what you need to do if we see a sasquatch."

Blizzard directed his dark-eyed stare at Noah, then tipped his head and growled.

"That's right, buddy," Noah answered. "You chew off its head."

A voice rose in Noah's ear: "Sounds great for you, Noah . . . but who's supposed to help me?"

"You got P-Dog, don't you?" Noah said.

Richie stared down at P-Dog, who was scurrying beside his feet, and shook his head. "A prairie dog. You get a polar bear, Ella gets a rhino, and I get a prairie dog."

"Not just *one* prairie dog," said a voice that Richie recognized as Ella's. "A whole bunch!"

"Is this your usual sarcasm?" Richie asked as he, Tameron, and the large coterie of prairie dogs rounded a bend in the tunnel by a curtain marked "Ostrich Island." "I can't really tell without seeing your face. Or has sarcasm become such a part of your personality that you forget when you're using it."

Ella just laughed, the bone mic carrying her cackle into the airwaves and the ears of the other Crossers.

Richie cursed Ella under his breath.

"I heard that," Ella said.

"What?" Richie said. "How?"

Richie heard Tank laughing, then the big man's voice rose in his head. "Don't forget . . . the bone mic picks up the vibrations in your skull, not the volume of your voice."

"Oops," Richie said. "Good thing it can't read my thoughts."

Tameron looked down at Richie. "Don't worry, kid. The Descenders—we got your back. That's one of the reasons we're here."

Richie nodded, and a wave of appreciation rolled over him. After what the scouts had gone through in the Secret Polliwog Bog, he was relieved to be walking beside a brawny teenager—especially one that could sprout a huge, crushing tail.

As the airwaves became silent, Richie turned his

attention to the prairie dogs around him again. They were scampering about, sniffing at clumps of dirt and half-buried rocks, their short, pointy tails whipping the air just above their wide rumps. Using their front paws, some climbed short ways up the walls to dab their moist snouts at interesting spots along the bricks. Richie was certain they were trying to pick up the scent of a sasquatch.

"Megan," Richie said, "how are you guys doing?"

Megan glanced at Hannah, then looked down at Podgy to find his beady black eyes in the dim tunnel light. The penguin seemed uninterested and unconcerned in his normal way. "We're somewhere in the west territory of the Grottoes, I think. No sign that sasquatches have been through here."

Tank's voice boomed in her ear. "Don't forget to look for tufts of hair—they're always falling out." After a few seconds, he added, "You guys getting the hang of the headsets?"

Megan nodded, realized Tank couldn't see her, then said, "Roger."

Ella said, "Roger, charlie, bravo, delta—prepare for takeoff" in what Megan thought was a perfect imitation of a male pilot. Megan smiled. Only her best friend could be making jokes at a time like this.

"Girl," Tank said, "you're about as goofy as they come."

"You know me and phonetic designation, Tank—I can barely help myself."

They continued on in silence for a bit. Megan, Podgy, and Hannah walked through a portal to an adjoining area of the Grottoes and appeared in a dark passage lined with gray cinder blocks. Water dripped from a few cracks in the flat ceiling, and mold grew in recessed spots. Bugs crawled along the walls, and the dank air seemed to press down on them.

From around a bend came three grizzly bears with heads as round as beach balls. Megan immediately realized they were Gifteds on patrol. As they moved past Megan, Podgy, and Hannah, the bears paid them little mind. One unintentionally swung its wide rump into Podgy, who teetered on one webbed foot and, with flailing flippers, barely avoided toppling over. Not long after the bears were gone, two lions pushed out from a curtain and padded down the tunnel. More Gifteds, Megan guessed.

As they walked by a thin stream of water falling from a ceiling crack, Megan reached up her palm and let water splash down on her fingers. Into her bone mic, she said, "It's pretty wet over here. Tank—you sure these tunnels are safe?"

"Safe as they've ever been," Tank answered. "You're probably near a bunch of portals to places with water. Sometimes water saturates the ground near the gateways.

We're not sure why it happens, but it's nothing to worry about."

Megan shook her head in amazement and swept her stare along the walls. All these tunnels that connected the Clarksville Zoo to the Secret Zoo . . . it still felt like something from a dream.

As the three Crossers rounded a new corner, Ella's voice rose in her ear: "Well, well . . ."

". . . well . . . Look who it is."

Richie spoke up: "I hope you're not looking at a sasquatch."

"Negative, Charlie Brown Bravo. I'm staring at our new pal, Punchy."

Hopping straight toward Ella were six kangaroos. As their hind legs heaved forward and back, the tips of their ears nearly swiped the ceiling. One of the kangaroos had an ear that was bent over sideways. Punchy.

Little Bighorn let out a snort and, to allow room for the kangaroos, stepped to one side of the tunnel, bumping into Ella, who brushed against his leathery skin and almost fell sideways. The rhino lowered his head and pointed his horn at the kangaroos in a protective, get-too-close-and-I'll-skewer-you way. As the kangaroos hopped past, they kept nervous stares locked on the horn. Punchy, the last to go by, cocked back one of his short forelimbs and then bopped the side of the rhino's head. In anger, Little Bighorn swung his snout around, his horn just missing the kangaroo's tailed rump.

"Yikes," Ella said.

"What's wrong?" Noah asked into the airwaves.

"Little Big . . . he almost made a shish kebab out of Punchy."

Ella swung her head around and watched the kangaroos disappear behind a bend in the tunnel.

Some time passed, and the airwaves stayed silent. Ella, Little Bighorn, and Solana passed a portal to Grottoes EW and another to Bear with Us! As Little Bighorn sniffed the ground, bursts of air shot through his nostrils and stirred clouds of dirt. Ella and Solana walked beside the big rhino and looked around for footprints or tufts of hair.

After an hour of searching, Tank called everyone back to the Grottoes beneath Butterfly Nets, the place they'd started. Richie was the last to return, and as he rounded a bend in the tunnel, the prairie dogs ran circles around his feet, nipping playfully at one another.

"Nobody saw nothing?" Tank asked once the full group of Crossers had gathered.

"Nope," Ella said. "Not a thing."

Megan and Noah shook their heads.

"Okay," Tank said. "Time to get you guys home. The rest of us will take it from here for now. You guys keep the headsets; just don't hide them in your underwear drawers so your parents find them when they're putting away laundry."

The scouts nodded. They said quick good-byes to their animal friends with pats of their hands, then walked to the tunnel branch that led to Butterfly Nets. At the base of the stairs, Noah stopped and turned back.

"Tank?" Noah said.

"Yeah?"

"The sasquatches . . . are they . . ." As Noah's voice trailed off, his stare shifted back and forth on the ground, as if he'd dropped his words and were trying to find them.

"What's up?" Tank spoke into Noah's awkward silence.

Noah lifted his gaze. "The outside world—*our* world— how much danger are we really in?"

The way Tank looked away from Noah made him nervous. He rubbed a spot on his bald head and said, "Sasquatches in the Grottoes . . . we've never seen anything like this. They've never gone this far."

Though Tank had done his best to avoid Noah's question, he'd answered it perfectly.

Noah nodded, turned again, and then led his friends up the stairs back into his neighborhood, a place that was under assault.

CHAPTER 21

GIRLS' NIGHT OUT

"What about Derek Johnson?"

"What *about* Derek Johnson?"

"You think he's cute?"

Ella thumbed through the photo book of her mind and stopped on a picture of Derek Johnson, a new fifth grader at Clarksville Elementary, then looked him over for a second.

"Nope." She fell silent and reconsidered. "A little bit, maybe. He's got those green eyes. And that hair. But are you asking me if he's Hollywood hot? Not a chance."

Megan smiled, but said nothing.

The two girls were lounging in Fort Scout, Megan in the beanbag, Ella lying on her back on the floor, her legs propped up on a chair. They were bundled up to protect themselves from the cold, and as they talked, their cloudy breath rose like steam. Noah was inside watching television, and Richie was at home. It was almost eight o'clock on Tuesday, just a day after the scouts had explored the Grottoes and practiced using their headsets. For the past hour, most of their conversation had been about the Secret Zoo—the sasquatches, the tarsiers, the Descenders. But their thoughts and words had finally drifted to lighter topics: life, school, and now a rare topic between the two of them—boys.

"What about Ryan?" Megan asked.

"Ryan Whalen?" Ella grunted. "Are you *kidding* me! He always has a little booger in his nose—have you noticed that?"

Ella could tell by the reach of Megan's smile that she had.

"Why he doesn't pick that thing . . . I have no idea. He's had that boog since, like, third grade."

The two of them broke out laughing, Megan so hard that she nearly rolled out the beanbag.

Megan threw out another name: "Jake?"

"Jake Peterson?"

Megan nodded, her pigtails wagging.

"I don't know," Ella said. "What about you?"

In a flash of the Christmas tree lights, Ella could see that Megan was blushing. Her friend, braver than anyone Ella knew, was shy about her feelings toward boys. Just the topic made her squirm.

Megan shrugged and nervously adjusted her glasses.

"Yes or no," Ella said. "I'm not letting you pass with a shrug this time."

Megan shifted in the beanbag. "Not really," she said at last.

Ella smiled. "'Not really' is a lot like 'a little bit.'"

Megan pulled her shoulders up to her ears.

"Not accepting shrugs," Ella reminded.

"Okay . . ." Megan blurted out. "A little bit, I guess."

Ella thought to tease her friend, then decided against it.

Megan asked, "What about Richie?"

"*Ohhh . . . emmm . . . geee . . .* Tell me you're not serious! *Richie!*"

Smiling, Megan said, "You have to pretend that he's not *our* Richie—just a guy on the streets, someone you've never met."

"And his nerdiness?"

"Gone," Megan said. "No big glasses. No pocketfull of pens."

Ella tried to imagine a Richie reduced to his bare looks. After a full minute, she shook her head, saying, "Nope.

I can't do it. Richie is Richie—all flood pants and flashy shoes. I can't see him any other way."

Megan clapped her hands once. "Me either!"

For a few minutes, the girls went on like that, discussing boys and the things that did or did not make them cute. For Ella, the topic, as always, felt strange and exciting—especially when sharing it with Megan. The two of them had been friends their whole lives. For years, they'd thought boys were the grossest things in the world. Now, they barely knew what to do with their new feelings.

"Do you want to get married?" Megan asked.

"Not in fifth grade," Ella teased, as she rose off the floor.

"Eventually, though?"

Ella sat at the table, turned to her friend, and watched the Christmas lights reveal Megan's sincerity. She scooped up one of Richie's electrical gadgets from the table, a tiny bulb affixed to a wire, and twirled it in her fingertips. "Richie and all his stuff . . . What is this thing?"

"I'm not accepting shrugs," Megan said, referring to how Ella was dodging the question.

As Ella turned over the question, images of her family appeared. She saw her mother, her father. She saw them together, then she saw them apart. She envisioned herself lying in bed at night, crying into her pillow. How long had this gone on? Weeks? Months? How long had she blamed herself for her parents' divorce? As Ella absently watched Richie's gadget spin across her fingertips, her stomach clenched and pain poked into her heart. She had long known that emotional hurt could become physical.

"No," Ella said, her tone flat and cold. "My mom said it best—marriage is momentary."

"It doesn't have to be," Megan shot back.

Ella considered this for a long time. At last, she said, "But who gets to decide?"

Ella lifted her gaze and watched Megan appear and disappear in consecutive flashes of light.

"How often do you think about him?" Megan asked.

"Every day," Ella answered. "My mom still cries at night. I don't."

"You shouldn't be afraid to."

Ella smiled, but there was anger in it. "It's easier to hate than it is to hurt."

"Ella, you can't—"

But Ella jumped out of her chair so suddenly that Megan's words stopped. She tossed down Richie's gadget, walked over to the table with the dancing snowman, and pressed his button. With a smile, she watched the three globes of his body shift and shake as the song played.

"We're just days away from Christmas," she said. "Let's stay in good cheer."

Megan nodded and forced a weak smile. She knew what all the scouts knew. Ella wasn't avoiding the topic of her father to spare herself the pain—she was doing it to spare her friends the pain.

"You're right about one thing," Megan said. She motioned to the snowman. "That thing . . . it's just the right amount of *perfectly annoying*."

Ella giggled to let Megan know it was okay to laugh, and then they both did. Ella pushed out her rump and rolled her hips from side to side in dead-on mimicry of the snowman. Megan laughed harder than ever and rolled around in the beanbag, chanting, "Woo! Woo!" and pumping her fist above her head in a hip-hop way as Ella danced around the fort.

As Ella strutted near a wall, she suddenly stopped as her gaze happened to fall upon something outside the window. In the porch light three houses down, something was moving around in her neighbor's backyard. But this something wasn't just *moving*—it was *hopping*. Ella dropped her hands to the windowsill and peered out to see a kangaroo. Somehow it had gotten beyond the zoo wall and was now jumping around, looking confused about how to get back.

"Megan!" Ella shouted. "Come here, quick!"

In what seemed less than a second, her friend was at her side, staring out.

"Oh my . . . What's it doing?"

"The Grottoes," Ella answered. "It must have gotten

confused in them and taken a wrong way out."

The kangaroo became startled by something and then headed off away from Fort Scout, its hind legs kicking up a thin cloud of snow. Within seconds, it was gone.

Megan turned her stare back and forth between Ella and the place the kangaroo had been, her pigtails whipping around like the beaded strings of a spinner drum.

"What do we do?" Megan asked.

"Exactly what we're supposed to do!" Ella answered.

With that, Ella ran across the fort, dropped down on the slide, and rode it to the ground. With Megan at her heels, she tore off across the Nowickis' yard in chase of the kangaroo.

CHAPTER 22

THE PURSUIT OF PUNCHY

"Which way?" Megan asked.

The two were running side by side across the Barkers' backyard. Twilight had long since dissolved into night, leaving little more than general shapes to see. Across the stretch of yards, Ella discerned the silhouettes of pools, sheds, and play sets. Occasional porch lights dotted the darkness and cast long shadows across brick walls and the snow-dusted grass. Leafless tree branches seemed to etch the sky.

"Straight, I guess!"

They jumped the hedge along the Barkers' property, Ella's toes skipping off the tips of their branches. As they swung a right turn in the Hunters' winding backyard, the kangaroo came into view along the dimmest reaches of a porch light. Ella noticed the way one of its ears bent to the side.

"You got to be kidding me!" Ella said. "That's Punchy!"

Punchy seemed to become scared by something. He jumped left, then right, his legs kicking out to the sides. Then he continued straight after bounding a large evergreen bush, his tail plowing through the branches and sending a puff of snow toward the sky.

"What are we going to do if we catch him?" Megan asked.

"I don't know," Ella admitted. "Tackle him?"

"Tackle him?"

"Maybe we can steer him back to the zoo. If he hopped the wall once, he can do it again."

As Ella heard the words come off her own lips, she realized it was the better plan. The scouts had learned a lot since crosstraining with the Descenders, but tackling a kangaroo wasn't something they'd practiced.

The girls were quickly gaining ground on Punchy, just two yards separating them. Ella felt the cold air swirling in her lungs, her ponytail slapping across her shoulders. Her earmuffs kept sliding off her ears, and she kept correcting them with swipes of her gloves. Each time she glanced at Megan, she noticed the way her friend's pigtails wagged up and down like the wings of a large bird.

The girls closed to within one yard. As they ran, Ella occasionally glanced into the houses that they passed. In many, dark rooms were filled with flickering lights as televisions played. In others, she saw people. She spotted Mrs. Parker standing at her kitchen window, doing something at the sink. She saw the Jeffersons on the couch, a tub of popcorn being passed between them. She saw Jessica Jones, a sixth grader at her school, gabbing into her cell phone while twirling her hair around a finger. Had anyone seen her and Megan in their mad dash through their dark yards? Ella could only hope not.

Punchy tried to jump through the middle of a play set and hooked one of his short forelimbs on a chain. He spun and crashed to the snowy grass, his long legs kicking at the nothingness of a world swept out from beneath him. Swings clattered and clanked, their metal chains ringing like chimes. He rolled himself upright and pushed his big feet against the ground. In the air, he squirmed his body back into position and continued on as if nothing had happened.

Within seconds, Ella and Megan closed in on the swing set. In an effort to save time, they chose to go through it rather than around it. With a turn of her shoulders and a buck of her hips, Ella twined her body through the bounce and throw of the chains. But as Megan ran beneath the play structure, a swing dropped sideways in front of her and she landed her waist across its bendable seat. Unable to slow down, she ran until the wide band of plastic conformed around her sides, the chains went taut, and she was lifted off her feet. She swung backward, her hands and knees pulling through the snow. When the swing reached the end of its backward throw, she was launched into the air. Her rear end struck the ground, and she slid through the grass like a character in a cartoon.

Ella ran back, grabbed Megan's hand, and hoisted her to her feet, saying, "Now you know what it feels like to be Richie."

Megan fixed her glasses and shook the confusion out of her head. Then the two girls navigated through the swings and started after Punchy again.

"Where is he?" Megan asked as they stormed into the Carters' backyard, barely dodging a concrete birdbath that seemed to rise out of nowhere in the darkness.

Ella shook her head. "I don't see him."

For the next two minutes, the girls charged down the path they hoped Punchy had taken. They stormed across the Smiths' brick patio, veered around the Campbells' shed, and beat across the planks of the Rogerses' gazebo, always keeping to the yards beside the concrete wall of the zoo's perimeter. Just when they feared they'd lost him, Punchy appeared in the colorful light being thrown from the eaves of the Stewarts' house, which was decked out for Christmas. As the lights blinked, Punchy looked red, then green, then red again.

"There he is!" Megan said, a gloved finger aimed in the kangaroo's direction.

Again, Ella glanced through the windows of the surrounding houses. Had anyone seen them? If so, no one had stepped outside or bothered to chase after them.

Punchy jumped out of the holiday glow of the Stewarts' place and landed in the Fergusons' yard, where he came upon an aboveground pool, a circular thing with blue walls and a tarp stretched across the top. Rather than go around it, he tried to go over it, and when he did, he slid across the tarp and the sheet of ice beneath it. His feet struck the opposite edge of the pool wall and he tumbled over the side, disappearing from view.

"Punchy!" Ella called out way too loudly.

Seconds later, the girls rounded the pool just as the frenzied kangaroo found his feet and hopped off again. Before he could get too far, Ella went into a headfirst dive and wrapped her hands around the tip of his tail. Punchy barely seemed to care. He hopped on, pulling Ella behind him.

Ella said, "Stop!" as her shoulders rocked up and down and her face repeatedly sank into the shallow snow.

As Ella was dragged, she felt her ankles being seized and realized Megan had jumped onto her. For a second they were both pulled through the snow; then their weight proved to be too much for Punchy, who fell forward, his snout banging against the ground.

Ella released Punchy's tail, and Megan let go of Ella's ankles. As the two girls climbed to their feet, Ella said, "Well . . . guess we know how to tackle a kangaroo now."

Punchy jumped up and spun around, coming face-to-face with Ella.

"It's us, you doofus!"

The kangaroo tipped his head to one side and seemed to study her. Even in the darkness, Ella could make out his dark eyes. The tip of his black snout was coated in snow.

"It's us," Megan repeated.

Punchy glanced at Megan, seemed to register who she was, then turned back to Ella. He looked her over and then threw a quick, unexpected jab into her chest.

"Ow!" Ella said. "You little . . ."

As Ella cocked her arm, Megan seized her wrist. "Don't" was all she said.

Ella uncoiled her fingers and let her arm drop. "You're right. The neighbor's yard . . . probably not the best place to start a fistfight with a kangaroo." Ella turned to Punchy. "I don't know what you're doing over here, but you need to be on the other side of"—she shot a finger toward the zoo wall—"that thing."

Punchy swung his snout toward the Clarksville Zoo and seemed to study it.

"C'mon," Ella said. She took off running toward the wall, waving one arm behind her. "This way."

Punchy and Megan fell in line behind her. As they ran away from the houses and into the wooded edges of the yards, Ella once again looked around and wondered if anyone had seen anything. She steered through the trees until she reached the zoo wall. The slab of pitted concrete stretched several feet above their heads. As Ella and Megan stopped, Punchy didn't. With a hard kick of his hind legs, he easily cleared the wall and dropped down behind it. The girls listened to his feet rustling the crisp, snowy leaves, and waited as the sound softened, then vanished altogether.

"He's gone," Megan said.

"Yeah," said Ella. "Some Gifted, huh? He hangs a wrong left and totally freaks out."

Megan said, "I hope the Secret Society knows what they're doing, putting all these animals in the Grottoes."

"And I hope that's the last time we have to chase a kangaroo through our neighborhood." Ella straightened her earmuffs and said, "C'mon, let's get home before Mrs. Ferguson looks out her window and realizes we're not lawn ornaments."

The two of them turned and headed back to Fort Scout, this time keeping to the cover of the trees.

❧ CHAPTER 23 ❧

THE BEGINNING OF THE END

Megan lay in bed tossing, getting tangled in the sheets. Every ten minutes or so, she'd peer at her bedside clock. Now it was almost one o'clock in the morning, two days after the Punchy incident. She kept thinking about the Grottoes, the Gifteds, and what had happened in the Secret Polliwog Bog. She kept seeing the clump of fur that Tank had shown them beneath the Knickknack and Snack Shack. How soon before the sasquatches attacked her neighborhood? Could they be stopped?

She wrestled out of bed and donned her glasses, hoping to rid herself of the images in her head. At the window, she looked out. The sky was starry and bright, the streets calm and quiet. A dusting of snow covered the grass. She peered out for the tarsiers and failed to spot them in the distant trees. Deciding that she needed a glass of orange juice, she crept out of her room and tiptoed down the hall, glancing through the half-open bedroom doors as she went. Everyone was asleep.

She walked down the stairs, crossed the kitchen, and went to the fridge, where she took out the juice and poured a glass. Sipping it, she gazed out the window at Fort Scout. Even in the bright night, it was impossible to see the Descender inside it.

She wondered who was posted in Fort Scout. Maybe she could sneak across the backyard and peek in. Maybe it would ease her mind and help her sleep. It would just take a minute.

"Forget it," she told herself. "Dumb idea."

She gulped the last of her juice and turned from the sink, intending to go upstairs. Instead she found herself walking to the back door, where she put on her jacket, her fleece headband, and her gloves. Without another thought, she slipped through the creaking door and eased it shut.

The wind stung her cheeks and swirled the powdery snow. She dashed across the yard and clambered up the ladder to Fort Scout. Pushing through the door, she discovered three Secret Cityzens: Sam, Marlo, and Podgy. Podgy was standing at the back of the fort, and Sam was kneeling beside the window, squinting into binoculars. Marlo, perched on the sill, spotted Megan and chirped.

Sam dropped the binoculars against his leg and stared at Megan. "You're joking, right?"

"I couldn't sleep," she said.

"And what? You thought you'd rest better out here in the freezing cold?"

Megan crossed the fort and knelt by Sam. Marlo jumped to her shoulder, chirped twice, then fluttered his wings. Podgy waddled over.

Looking at Podgy, Megan said, "I can honestly say that I never expected to sit in this tree fort with a penguin. Never, ever." Ideas and emotions swirled inside her like beads in the bowl of a kaleidoscope.

"You guys hear about the change of plans?" Sam asked as he hoisted his binoculars again and stared through them.

"Change of plans?" Megan repeated.

"Yeah. The Gifted in the Grottoes—gone for now."

"Seriously?"

"Too dangerous. What happened with Punchy a few nights ago—the Secret Council was tripping out."

"What about your best Gifteds? Can't you guys keep a few in?"

Sam slowly swung his binoculars over to a new spot. "Council has it under review. For now, it's just us and the usual animals—the ones that we've trained to do this."

Megan opened her mouth to say more and then closed it again. She stared at the floor and considered this. Was this a good thing? Or did it put her world in more danger?

"What about the other Descenders?" she finally asked. "You guys said there's a whole bunch besides you four."

Sam shook his head. "That's under review, too. Right now, they're wrapped up in their own business, guarding the city gateways. We can't take them off post."

Megan stayed quiet and considered this. Was it better to keep more guard on the City of Species or her neighborhood? She didn't know.

Podgy, perhaps sensing Megan's concern, waddled closer to her. Megan hugged him briefly with one arm and allowed a smile onto her lips.

After some time, Megan asked, "Have you seen anything weird?"

"Not yet," Sam said. "But the night's young."

For about ten minutes, the two of them chatted about things. They discussed the patrols, the tarsiers, and the Grottoes. As they talked, Marlo swung his beak back and forth between them, as if following the conversation. Just as Megan was about to ask a question about Mr. Darby, Sam raised his hand, stopping her. He fixed his stare on the floor and touched two fingertips to his ear. His body froze, and his eyes shifted nervously. Someone was talking into his headset.

"How many?" he asked.

Podgy began to rock back and forth. Marlo paced along Megan's shoulder, his tiny talons pricking her jacket. Megan studied Sam and tried to read the emotions on his face.

"Roger," he said. "Out."

"What is it?" Megan asked.

Sam dropped his fingers from his earpiece and faced her. Marlo jumped back to the windowsill, where he hopped around, chirping wildly. Podgy rushed to the open door and stared out at the zoo.

"Sam, what's wrong?"

"Sasquatches," he managed to say. "Charlie spotted them. They're roaming inside Creepy Critters. And at least one is out—loose in the zoo."

Megan gasped and stared out at the Clarksville Zoo. She spotted the distant dark rooftop of Creepy Critters. Somewhere inside it, sasquatches were tramping down the halls.

The binoculars slipped from Sam's grasp and clunked on the wood planks. The Descender shook the confusion from his head and jumped into action.

"Marlo," he said. "Get Ella, then Richie. Make sure they know it's an emergency."

The kingfisher sprang off the windowsill into the night sky.

"Megan, I need you to get inside and wake up your brother. Make sure—"

But before Sam could finish, Podgy had leaped to the frame of the open window and hurled himself into the air. Stroking his flippers, he sank like a rock. Then, just when he seemed certain to slam down, he flew in a straight line, inches off the ground. Across the yard he went, his round belly swirling the powdery snow. He reached the house and swept up along the wall to Noah's second-story room, landing in a wide flower box on the window ledge.

"Forget that," Sam told Megan. "Podgy's already on it." He shot her a glance and seemed to detect her apprehension. "Megan, I need you to be sharp. Are you sharp?"

"I . . . I think so," said Megan.

"Don't think," Sam shouted. "*Know!* We need you right now—we need all the scouts!"

"But what about the Descenders guarding the gateways?" Megan asked. "Can we—"

"They got their hands full. The sasquatches . . . right now they're hitting the City of Species."

Megan's head spun. High in a tree fort filled with unimaginable guests, she suddenly felt certain she was witnessing the beginning of the end.

CHAPTER 24

THE PLUMMET WITH PODGY

Noah heard tapping on his window and sat up with a jerk. He threw his legs over the bed and glanced at the clock: 1:16 A.M.

The tapping came again.

"Marlo?" said Noah, thinking that the messenger bird was responsible for the noise. He dashed across the room and threw open the drapes, expecting to find the blue bird. But what he instead discovered shocked him into taking two steps back. Filling most of the window was a penguin—an enormous emperor penguin, its flippers pressed against its sides, its bill tipped upward, its webbed feet flattening the limp remains of Noah's mother's summer flowers. Podgy.

Noah threw open the window, allowing the cold night air to invade the room.

"What's wrong?"

Podgy spun around in the flower box, his flat feet slinging snowy dirt across the floor of the room, and presented his back to Noah. He wanted Noah to climb on.

Noah gasped. "Podgy, there's no way! My parents—"

The penguin jumped and brought his feet down hard, shaking the box and rattling the shutters. His point was obvious. Noah was needed, and there was no time to waste.

Noah had a vision of his mother walking into his room several hours from now to find his bed empty and his window open. This would surely force him to tell his parents about the Secret Zoo. What would that mean to the Secret Society? To the safety of the world?

Podgy jumped once more, shaking the box and rattling the siding.

"This is crazy!" Noah went to his bedroom door and softly closed it. He stripped off his pajamas, then grabbed yesterday's wad of clothes off the floor and climbed into them. "Man, I hope you know what you're doing." He put on a jacket, shoes, and his red hunting cap. Fully dressed, he walked back to the window and considered how to climb onto Podgy. There was no way the flower box would hold his weight and Podgy's at the same time.

"How about I meet you at the front door?"

Podgy began to rock in place, his webbed feet crushing flower stems and leaving penguin tracks in the dirt. After a few seconds of this, he wagged his flippers up and down.

Noah had spent enough time with Podgy to know what he wanted, which was for Noah to jump onto his back, hurling them both out of the flower box and into the air.

"You got to be kidding me," Noah muttered as he backed all the way to the far wall. He stared at Podgy and the open window across the room and became certain that this wasn't a good idea.

"Here goes," Noah said.

Without another thought, he took off running. He jumped out the window, wrapping his arms around Podgy and knocking the two of them forward. Flowerbed dirt spilled everywhere as they dropped toward the ground, Podgy wagging his flippers. A second before they crashed, Podgy flew out of the fall and swept across the yard, his stomach again brushing the snowy grass. Noah lay stretched across his back, his legs dangling behind the penguin, his feet skipping over the ground.

With a swift upward turn, Podgy rose three feet, five feet, eight feet, more. As he soared near Fort Scout, two figures came into view: Megan and Sam. They leaned out the window, marveling at the sight of Noah and Podgy. Noah wondered what his sister was doing in Fort Scout, then dismissed his concern. Surely Megan had the greater question: Why was Noah flying across their yard on a penguin in the middle of the night?

Podgy looped around the big oak, swerving over and under the longer branches. As he returned to the front, Noah again spotted his sister leaning out the window, her jaw hanging open, her pigtails sticking out. Points of moonlight shone in the otherwise dark lenses of her glasses. Podgy veered away from the tree and cut across the yard, heading for the concrete wall.

Noah had once believed this wall merely divided his neighborhood from an ordinary zoo. Now he understood much more. The wall divided two worlds, Noah's and another, a place where animals walked beside humans in a city built upon the trees. Filled with majesty, promise, and peril, this other world was known as the Secret Zoo.

As Podgy soared over the wall, Noah braced himself for anything.

❦ CHAPTER 25 ❦

ELLA WAKES UP

When Ella heard the tapping on her window, she threw off the covers and sat up at the edge of her bed. The clock on her nightstand read 1:17. Something was wrong. She rushed to the window and peered through a slit in the blinds. Standing on the outside sill was Marlo. Their eyes met, and the bird opened and closed his beak with a chirp that was muted by the glass.

Ella threw open the blinds and then the window, prompting Marlo to flap his wings in a fuss. Something wasn't just wrong—something was *terribly* wrong.

"What is it?" Ella asked.

The kingfisher dove into the air, flew in a tight circle, then landed back on the sill. He repeated this pattern again and again.

"The zoo? Do you need us?"

Marlo jumped up a few inches and landed with a chirp.

Ella's eyes widened. She gazed toward the zoo, but could see nothing other than her neighborhood houses, their windows dark, their occupants fast asleep. She looked toward the trees and the tarsiers in them. Nothing.

She turned back to Marlo. "Okay. Go wake Richie. Tell him I'm on my way."

Marlo chirped twice, sprang into the air, and dissolved into the night.

She closed her window, dressed, then tiptoed from her bedroom. In the hallway, she heard her mom snoring. If she were to wake and find her missing, Ella would be dead. At the door to the garage, she donned her jacket and earmuffs. As she slipped out, she reached for the button to open the door and stopped herself. Too loud. She opted for the small door to the backyard and grabbed her bicycle on the way.

Outside, she climbed on the bike and pedaled across the snowy lawn. Once on the street, she raced to Richie's house, wondering what could be wrong at the zoo. But didn't she already know? Yes, she was certain she did. She'd only seen Marlo so crazed once before—the day he'd spotted sasquatches charging from the caves of the Dark Lands. Now, they were escaping from the Grottoes.

Certain that her world was under attack, Ella stood on her pedals and pumped her legs with all her might.

CHAPTER 26

RICHIE RIDES AGAIN

Tap . . . tap . . . tap.

Richie bolted upright, making his bedsprings groan.

"Wha— Who's there?"

Tap . . . tap.

He swept his fingers along his nightstand until they bumped into his glasses. When he threw them on, the blurry view of the glowing clock digits came into focus: 1:17. He glanced at the window bug-eyed and confused.

Tap! Tap! Tap! Tap! Tap!

He erupted from the bed and rushed over to the window, where he pulled open the blinds. Perched on the outside sill was Marlo. He stared up at Richie, his head cocked to one side. Then he leaned forward and pinged his beak against the glass again.

Richie flinched, then slid open the window. Marlo danced around, chirping wildly.

"What's— What are you—"

Richie saw something moving up the snow-dusted street. Someone was racing toward his house on a bicycle. As he peered out, Marlo turned with a jump toward the shadowy figure. Richie realized it was Ella.

"What in the world?"

Ella veered off the street at a dangerous speed and bounced across Richie's yard, nearly crashing into a bare bush surrounded by the litter of its own leaves. She bumped her way to the house and skidded to a stop, her rear tire sliding on the snowy grass.

Staring up at Richie, Ella boomed, "It's the sasquatches!"

Totally confused, Richie stayed silent.

"They're getting out—I'm sure of it!"

"How do—"

Ella waved Richie down. "Come on! We got to go!"

"*What?* My parents—what if—"

"I think they'd rather find you out of bed than find a sasquatch lounging in their porch swing!"

On the windowsill, Marlo chirped once, siding with Ella.

Richie gave in. "Okay. I'm coming."

He closed the window, dressed quickly, then stepped gingerly past his parents' bedroom. At the front door, he slipped into his running shoes, jacket, and hat, then went out onto the front porch. From around the corner of the house, Ella pedaled up to him.

"You got your bike?" she asked.

"Nuh-uh. It's downstairs for the winter."

"Then get on," she instructed.

Richie looked her bike over. "On where? Your head?"

"The handlebars."

"Yeah, right."

"Richie! If there was ever a time to be brave, this is it. Now get on!"

Ella was right. If the sasquatches were storming out of the Grottoes, there was no other choice. He piled onto the bike, his skinny rear end dangling over the handlebars. Marlo swooped down and landed on his cap beside the pom-pom, which was twice as big as he was.

"*Oww!*" Richie shifted on the handlebars. "Something's poking my butt."

"Quit squirming!" Ella said. "And hold on. I'm going to make this trip in record time."

As she forced her weight onto the pedals, the bike slowly began to move. The handlebars jerked from side to side, the bike veering in all directions.

"*Stay still!*" Ella said.

"But my butt . . ." Richie protested.

"No buts! I don't want to hear about either one of them!"

As the bike gained speed, it became easier for Ella to control the handlebars and manage Richie's weight. She crossed the yard and turned onto the street, pedaling faster and faster.

"Be careful!" Richie commanded.

Ella's lack of response made him nervous.

As Ella, Richie, and Marlo raced toward the zoo, Richie became more and more afraid about what they might find there.

THE WINGS OF THE DESCENDER

Seeing Podgy fly into the zoo, Sam brushed past Megan and out the door of the fort.

"Let's go," he said.

Megan dropped her thoughts and chased the Descender onto one of the rope bridges. Sam crossed the shaky planks and stepped onto a lookout platform on a distant tree. He stopped and turned to Megan, who halted so suddenly that the bridge swayed beneath her feet.

Megan stood in the sag of the rope bridge, a few feet lower than Sam. With his back to the moon, his face was masked in shadow. For a moment, Sam did nothing but stare down on her. Then he raised his arms over his head and brought them back down, striking the zippers on his wrists against the buckles on his hips. He swept up his arms, ripping open rows of metal teeth that crisscrossed his jacket. Silver feathers, freed from their leathery confines, fell from his arms and sprouted from his sides. Thin rods telescoped out from the ends of his sleeves, dropping feathers neatly into place across a wide wingspan.

The Descender stood on the platform, his arms raised, his feathers swaying in the wind, moonlight outlining his body. Each wing stretched at least five feet past his usual reach. As he swung one arm toward Megan, the group of feathers waved like a freakish flag. He curled his fingers toward himself, a gesture for her to approach.

Megan instinctively took a step back. The bridge rocked.

"Megan, we need to."

The sound of her name carried by Sam's voice helped to humanize him again. She took a step forward, but then stopped.

"C'mon—we don't have time for this!" He waved her forward with his entire arm, his feathers fluttering and snapping.

She forced herself to cross the bridge. On the lookout platform, Sam towered above her like a thing from a daydream. He turned away, sweeping his arm over Megan, brushing his feathers along her body. With his back to her, he fell to one knee and leaned forward, dropping his wings.

"Get on."

Megan hesitated. "But I don't think—"

"Don't think. Just do."

She considered this and then leaned against Sam, wrapping her arms over his shoulders.

"Just don't fall off, and I'll do the rest."

He squatted on the platform, gathering strength in his legs. Then he sprang up and away from the tree. His massive wings shot out and began to row through the air. He swerved toward the zoo, Megan's body rolling and bucking as she lay across his silver feathers.

Megan peered over Sam's shoulder and watched the concrete wall pass beneath them. Then she looked out across the neighborhood. In nearly all the houses, the lights were out. She could only hope that some sleepless mother wouldn't glance out a window and spot her and Sam flying through the sky. Would the darkness and distance disguise them as a huge bird? Would the mother think her weary eyes were playing tricks on her? Megan could only hope for the best.

As they soared over the exhibits, animals stared up at them. Megan saw the stunned gazes of bears and wolverines. Even in the magical realm that the animals knew,

Megan and Sam were a sight to behold.

Coasting now on his wide wingspan, Sam carried Megan deep into the zoo. Though they hadn't discussed their purpose, it was obvious to Megan. They were hunting for the sasquatch that had escaped Creepy Critters. Megan's intention was to capture, but she knew Sam's was different.

Sam's intention was to kill.

✿ CHAPTER 28 ✿

A PATH TO AVOID

Racing through a stop sign on Phlox Drive, Ella hung a sharp right onto Zinnia Street, but with Richie mounted to the handlebars, she couldn't turn soon enough, and the bike careened into the Hugheses' yard. She tore through a lifeless garden of flowers, exploding wilted petals into the air. Richie thrashed about, his skinny rear end bouncing off the steel bar, the gearshift, and the pointy knobs of Ella's knees.

"Owww!" he squealed. "My butt! My butt! My butt!"

Marlo, still perched on Richie's hat, took issue with the shaky pom-pom beside him. It kept crashing into him, prompting the kingfisher to peck angrily at the offending ball of yarn.

Ella realized she could save time if she continued straight, cutting across the Hugheses' backyard and then through the Wilhelms' property, where she could rejoin the street. To gain speed, she raised herself up from the seat and bounced her weight on the pedals.

"Hold on, Richie!"

But Richie had only a single concern: *"My buuttt!"*

She sped around the side of the house and bounced onto a backyard patio. Glancing at the windows, she saw the lights were out. She wondered what Mrs. Hughes would think if she were to look out and find Ella tearing across her snowy patio on a bicycle with Richie sprawled across the handlebars, yelling about his rear end while a bird pecked angrily at his hat. Certainly she wouldn't be able to categorize it as an everyday sight.

Ella steered around a shed in the back reaches of the yard, then sped across the Wilhelms' lawn, crashing through several bushes and clipping a ceramic garden gnome, which lost its cone-shaped hat and the better part of its big nose. She bounced back onto the road, narrowly avoiding a rusted-out pickup truck. She leaned forward and pedaled with all her might. Marlo continued his assault on Richie's pom-pom, and Richie continued his daffy proclamations about his bottom.

Ella sped down the sidewalk on Walkers Boulevard and turned into the zoo parking lot. Except for a few cars, it was empty. She quickly neared the front gates, where a guard, recognizing Ella and Richie, leaped from his booth and kicked open a squealing gate. The guard waved them through with exaggerated sweeps of his arm. Ella zoomed past him, bawling out her thanks.

She turned onto the main path. In no time, the three of them passed Flamingo Fountain and rolled deeper into the zoo. As they sped by the exhibits, Ella didn't see anything out of the ordinary—certainly nothing that would have caused the panic she'd seen in Marlo. But minutes later, as they neared Creepy Critters, a sasquatch lunged out of the shadows and onto the path directly in front of them.

As the monster swung at them, Ella leaned to one side, intentionally dropping the bike. Claws whooshed through the air, just missing her head. The bike slammed into the legs of the sasquatch, tumbling the beast to the ground.

Ella's head smacked the concrete. Her eyes filled with stars, and a squeal erupted in her ears. The world clouded out. She lay on the path, too hurt to move, her cheek pressing against the cold concrete, blood trickling from her nose. Marlo jumped in front of her face, chirping wildly and fanning his wings. From her perspective, he seemed gigantic—larger than the distant buildings.

Forcing her head to rise, Ella spotted Richie. He was rolling on the ground, clutching his knees in pain. Next to him, the sasquatch lay in a heap, its legs tangled in the twisted frame of the wrecked bike.

Just as Ella hoped that the sasquatch had been knocked unconscious, the beast lifted its head. Then it looked around and fixed its stare directly on her.

CHAPTER 29

A Bird's-eye View

Podgy and Noah soared between the light of the stars and the lights of the zoo. As they neared the Forest of Flight, they skirted its domed roof. The glass panes blurred into a single piece, circular and unending. Noah saw his reflection in them: arms outstretched, jacket fluttering, legs dangling. He saw Podgy, too, his flippers stroking the air, his beak jutting forward, his belly sagging. Flying only a few feet from the gleaming rooftop, Noah couldn't resist the urge to reach out and touch it. His fingers skipped and squeaked along the glass.

Through the glass, Noah spotted tall trees, spills of

water, clouds of mist, and rocky mountainsides. The Forest of Flight contained the things from the natural world; those that couldn't be collected had been created.

Birds perched on branches and stood on the grassy floor. They raised their heads to watch Noah and Podgy pass. Noah wondered if any remembered him from his first supernatural encounter with the exhibit. How many had been there when the cloud of birds engulfed him? How many had helped him rescue his sister despite the risk?

Once Podgy had half circled the roof, he swooped away from the Forest of Flight. The wind rushed against them, noisily gathering in Noah's ears. From this height, Noah had a plain view of many exhibits: the bulky buildings of Metr-APE-olis; the towers of Koala Kastle; the zigzagging corridors of Creepy Critters.

In the distance, Noah saw the rooftops of the neighborhood. Inside houses, people slept, perhaps dreaming of fairy tale moments as incredible as the one Noah was living. In a way, he felt sorry for them. Even with the danger that the scouts now faced, Noah doubted he'd trade his position with anyone in the world. The wonder was sometimes worth the risks.

To the right, something suddenly soared above a stand of trees and headed straight toward them. Noah almost slipped off Podgy in shock at what he saw.

CHAPTER 30

FLIGHT OR FIGHT

Toward the middle of the zoo, Sam and Megan came upon a group of particularly tall trees. The Descender swerved upward, his body as vertical as the trunks, then sailed across the treetops, his wings stirring their branches. Once past the woods, he coasted downward, leveling out at around twenty feet from the ground. In front of them were Podgy and Noah. In silhouette, they looked like black-and-white animation brought to life from a children's comic: Podgy stroking his flipper wings; Noah clinging to his back, the earflaps of his cap fluttering.

As the duos neared each other, they veered in the same

direction to fly side by side. Sprawled across a penguin that had only recently learned to fly, Noah looked surprisingly relaxed. He flashed a smile, which Megan bounced back.

Megan said, "Is this nuts, or what?"

"It's like a dream!"

"It's got to be a dream, right? Any second now, Ma's going to wake me up for breakfast!"

"If she does, tell her I want pancakes!"

They laughed. For a moment, there was no flying penguin, no winged teenager, and no danger. All that existed was a special fondness that siblings shared, something that was normally kept buried in the day-to-day frustrations of living together.

The four of them swerved around trees and buildings. With each stroke of Sam's wings, a gust of wind lifted the earflaps of Noah's hat. As they crossed Arctic Town, Noah pointed to the Polar Pool and shouted for everyone to look. There was Blizzard, striding up the staircase to the underwater tunnel. He'd gotten out of his exhibit, undoubtedly using the same secret passage that he'd used to deliver Megan's note to the scouts not so long ago. From the air, Blizzard somehow looked more enormous than ever. When he reached the top of the stairs, he craned his long neck all around, likely trying to spot the sasquatch.

Megan cupped a hand to her mouth and hollered, "Blizzard! Up here!"

The bear raised his thick snout. Even in the darkness Megan could make out the black dot of his nose. Blizzard tipped back his head and roared, his voice muted by the wind in her ears.

"Follow us!" called Noah.

Blizzard padded onto a sidewalk and chased after them. His massive body rocked with such force that Megan almost expected the concrete to shatter under his feet.

The four continued to fly over the zoo, scanning the grounds. Animals had left their exhibits to stand guard. Megan saw lions hiding in bushes, monkeys staring out from trash cans, and meerkats peeking from waterspouts.

As they soared over Creepy Critters, Megan spotted something that made her gasp. She pointed at the ground, where Ella and Richie were lying on the sidewalk. Barely moving, they were clearly hurt. Beside them, a sasquatch lay tangled in the twisted frame of a bicycle.

"Podgy—go!" commanded Noah.

Podgy dove. Sam plunged after him, his wings pressed against his sides.

Below them, the sasquatch staggered to its feet, snapping the frame of the bicycle like a twig. It tossed the twisted pieces of metal aside and hobbled over to Ella. As the beast neared the fallen scout, it lifted an arm, spread its claws, and prepared to deliver a blow that would surely end her life.

﹇ CHAPTER 31 ﹈

LIGHTS OUT

Ella rolled over on her stomach. Her ears rang. Points of light flashed in her vision. She rose to her knees and tried to focus on the sasquatch. Its fangs curled over its lips; moonlight gleamed on its claws.

She knew that at any second those claws would come down on her. She thought that closing her eyes would make it easier to die. But before she could block out the sight of the sasquatch, something else did. The lights in the Clarksville Zoo suddenly blinked out. In groups of five or six, they went black—the lights in lampposts, on buildings, inside exhibits. Within seconds, darkness had engulfed the landscape.

✒ CHAPTER 32 ✑

More Surprises

With the zoo lights out, Noah used the moonlight to pinpoint the sasquatch. As the penguin went into his final dive, Noah kicked out his leg, connecting his foot squarely against the monster's forehead. Several things happened at once: the sasquatch roared in pain and fell backward; Podgy crashed to the ground; and Noah was thrown onto the snowy grass, where he slid and rolled until finally coming to a stop.

Noah stood and peered through the darkness. He made out the sasquatch lying on its back, writhing in pain, and the faint silhouettes of Megan and Sam, who had touched down on the sidewalk about fifty feet behind the fallen monster. Sam stepped away from Megan and ran at the sasquatch, his wings snapping open like sheets in a stiff wind. He lunged forward and flew parallel to the side-walk, no higher than three feet up. When he reached the sasquatch, he swept his legs beneath him, and talons—or something that looked like talons—sprang from his shoes. He snagged the beast by its leg and veered into the air, dragging along his captive, who writhed and kicked, trying to get free.

The Descender carried the sasquatch higher and higher. Noah followed their dark silhouette against the lighter backdrop of the sky. At around sixty feet, Sam opened his talons and his prisoner fell, its limbs flailing and kick-ing and grasping at the emptiness around it. It dropped behind a clump of trees and slammed soundlessly into the earth. Sam turned back in a graceful sweep, his wings seeming to brush the star-spotted canvas of sky. As Noah watched, words that he'd once read from the pages of the dictionary filled his head: *To pounce upon. To attack with violence and suddenness. To descend.*

Noah rushed over to Ella and Richie. Both scouts were standing, but with difficulty. He grabbed Ella's shoulders and studied her face.

"How bad are you hurt?"

Ella was too dazed to speak. With trembling hands,

she straightened her earmuffs, fluffed her ponytail, and wiped her nose, smearing blood across her cheek. Megan appeared and hugged Ella, almost knocking her off her feet. Noah held them steady and looked at Richie.

"Richie—you okay?"

Everything about Richie was crooked: his hat, his glasses, his jacket, his stance. Even his pants had shifted sideways. Noah went to his friend and tried to fix him—a tug here, a pull there.

"Richie?" he said again.

Rubbing his eyes, Richie glanced at Noah. "I . . ."

"Yeah?" said Noah. "What is it?"

"I got a joke," said Richie.

"You can't be serious."

Richie nodded, sending tremors through the pom-pom on his cap. In a shaky voice, he said, "What's . . . what's the difference between a sasquatch and a brick wall?"

"I have no idea."

"At full speed on Ella's bike—nothing."

Noah straightened Richie's glasses and nodded. "Not too horrible, given the circumstances."

Sam touched down nearby and folded his massive wings against his back as he shuddered to a stop. The tips of the wings trailed behind him like a cape. Among the shadows, he looked eerie.

"The talons," Noah said. "How . . . ?"

Sam picked up one foot and thrust it forward, launching steel hooks from the sole of his boot, three from his toes and one from his heel. They were smeared with blood. When he tucked his foot back, the hooks retracted.

Sam asked, "Everyone okay?"

They nodded.

Marlo touched down on Noah's shoulder, startling him.

"Marlo," said Noah. "We need help. Find Blizzard and Little Bighorn and bring them here."

With a chirp, Marlo sprang into the air.

Podgy waddled close, moving his gaze over the other Crossers.

To Noah, Sam said, "There are more sasquatches in Creepy Critters—Charlie spotted them."

Everyone stared at the exhibit. Perhaps forty yards away, it was perfectly dark, inside and out.

Noah said, "What do we—"

Sam held up his hand, silencing Noah. The Descender had his stare locked on the main entrance to Creepy Critters, a pair of glass doors standing on a wide concrete porch.

"I hear something," he said at last.

The scouts inched forward and listened. They kept silent. Around them, the wind moaned. They watched. A dusting of snow swirled over the eaves of the building.

Noah heard a muffled thud. Then another.

"Is that—"

Before he could finish, the main entrance to Creepy Critters burst outward. The glass doors shattered and snapped off their metal frames, their twisted remains hanging limply. Sasquatches jumped onto the wide porch, kicking over empty flowerpots. One sasquatch ripped out a staircase railing and hurled it into a nearby tree. Another smashed its fist through a window, sending shards of glass flying. The crowd of sasquatches quickly turned around and disappeared back into the dark building.

"What are they doing?" Noah asked.

Sam stared into the empty spot where the sasquatches had been. "No one expected this."

"Expected what?"

After what seemed like a long silence, Sam muttered, "They're clearing a path."

"For who?"

"The animals inside Creepy Critters . . . the sasquatches are releasing them."

Noah's heart dropped. Beside him, Richie gasped.

Into his headset, Sam said, "Charlie, I need all available units to report to Creepy Critters. Repeat—we need help!"

The scouts looked at Sam for direction. When it became

obvious that he'd suddenly been stunned into silence, it was Noah who took control.

"C'mon!" Noah said. "We got to go!"

Then he charged toward the exhibit—toward the black unknown and the monsters dwelling inside of it.

CHAPTER 33

DANGERS IN THE DARKNESS

Noah ran up the stairway to the entrance of Creepy Critters, where shards of glass and metal pieces lay all around. The dark, doorless entrance yawned like the mouth of a monster. He stepped through, debris crunching beneath his feet.

Inside, it was pitch-black. If the building had emergency lighting, it wasn't working. He tried to recall the exhibit from previous visits. He knew that in front of him stretched a long hallway. Twice as wide as the ones in his school, it had countless aquariums set in its walls. It led to a great room in the center of the building, known as the Creepy Core, from which other halls branched off, zigzagging and threading through one another like the passages of a maze.

The swampy odor of soil, mildew, water, and fish hung in the air. Without electricity and the usual noises of filters and bubbles, the exhibit was eerily quiet. Other than an occasional croak, hiss, or rattle, there was no sound.

Noah reached his hand back, intending to wave his group inside, only to have his wrist seized by something hiding in the darkness. Before Noah could yelp, a hand pressed over his mouth.

A voice spoke softly in his ear. "Don't panic. It's us." Noah knew the person the voice belonged to. Tameron. Slowly, the Descender removed his hand.

In a hushed voice, Noah asked, "How'd you get in?"

"Back door," Tameron whispered. "We were standing right here when the sasquatches busted out the main entrance, but we weren't coordinated enough to attack."

"Are the others here?" Noah asked. "Solana—you here?"

"Yeah," the darkness answered.

"And Hannah?"

To his left, Noah heard the soft *pop* of Hannah's chewing gum.

Tameron's silhouette appeared in the doorway. Noah saw his armored helmet and the start of his long tail. The Descender waved for Sam and the other scouts to come forward. In seconds, everyone was inside the building.

In a voice that was much too loud, Richie said, "Man, it's dark in here!"

"Shhh!" Ella scolded him in a whispered yell. "I know we're not as smart as you, but I'm pretty sure we all figured that out."

Sam asked Tameron, "Could you tell which way the sasquatches went?"

"Down to the Core, then to the right."

"Makes sense."

"How come?" asked Noah.

"That's where Gator Falls is—the alligator exhibit. It has the biggest portal in here to the Secret Zoo. Could be big trouble if the sasquatches bust it open."

The group fell silent. No one had any doubts about what they were up against.

Noah heard Sam move to the front of everyone. "Let's go. Stay close and stay quiet." His footsteps faded as he headed into the darkness.

They all followed, treading lightly. Noah held his arms out in front of him, feeling the space to ensure it was empty. Occasionally, he'd brush Ella, whom he was trailing, her soft ponytail sweeping across his fingers.

Noah strained to see something—anything. With no windows to the outside world, the darkness was absolute.

As he moved, he had no idea how much distance he had covered or how much he had yet to go.

Sensing their passage, the animals in the aquariums seemed to become anxious. They began to croak and squeak and rattle. Tails splashed above water; hard shells tapped against glass.

Noah used the sounds, their volume and direction, to measure his surroundings. He calculated the width of the hall, the height of the ceiling, the empty distance around him. In his head, he formed a faint image of the building.

Perhaps a minute into the walk, some sounds grew softer and others faded away altogether. The hallway was gone—Noah could hear its absence—which meant they'd moved into the Creepy Core. Noah lifted its image from his memory. It was as much as seventy-five feet across, and its walls held up a low, domed roof made of cement. Thick glass acted as a clear ceiling to section off the dome, creating an overhead aquarium. It was full of spiders. Some were small and lanky, and others had bodies as round and plump as grapes. Though the space was crowded with branches and leafy plants, spiders could always be seen crawling across the glass.

Sam whispered, "Which hallway is Gator Falls in?"

When no one responded, Noah took a chance. "I think it's three hallways down from where we're standing."

"We need a light," said Megan.

"Richie . . ." Ella whispered. "Your nerd-gear . . . Do you have your penlight?"

Richie loudly explored his pocket. "Yes. Everything's accounted for."

"Hold on," said Tameron. "No lights. We got sasquatches in here, and—"

"What would you rather do?" Ella said. "Stand here until we get trampled by bugs and animals? No thanks."

Tameron stayed silent. After a moment, he said, "Sam, what do—"

The building filled with the sound of breaking glass. In one of the branching halls, an aquarium had shattered. Noah spun to his right. He peered out and tried to pull an image out of the darkness. Nothing. Glass continued to clink against the floor. Then, all at once, the noises stopped. The fresh silence was terrifying.

"What was that?" someone gasped.

A response came, but not from anyone in their group. Far down a hall came a low, rumbling growl—the unmistakable sound of an alligator. It was followed by another, and another. Then there was a hiss and the crash of a body against a wall.

"Gator Falls," Sam said. "It's open."

Something grunted—something nearby. It had been an animal sound, quick and deep. Noah glanced around but couldn't see a thing. The animal grunted again, louder this time.

Something passed by Noah, and a long clump of hair brushed his hand. He yelped and pulled away, his eyes dancing as he tried in vain to raise an image in the darkness.

"Something's here!" he said.

"Richie!" said Sam. "Go ahead—use your penlight!"

A bloodcurdling scream filled Noah's head. Someone spun around and knocked him into someone else. This person jostled back, and for a few seconds Noah was bounced around like a pinball. When the shriek came a second time, Noah realized it was Solana.

"Richie—your light!" Sam commanded.

A narrow beam suddenly severed the darkness. It jerked in different directions until it landed on Solana, revealing of scene of such horror that Noah felt his insides turn.

A sasquatch was dragging Solana down the hall toward Gator Falls.

CHAPTER 34

CHAOS IN CREEPY CRITTERS

As Richie squirmed in fear, the beam of his flashlight jumped around, streaking the air and revealing the sasquatch like the flashes of a strobe light. As the monster backed down the hall, Solana's quills sprang from her jacket and stabbed deep into its body. Howling in pain, it released the Descender, who then slid down it, burying the spikes into its legs. The sasquatch lurched backward and swiped at its chest, tearing out the quills.

"Move!" Sam commanded.

Richie moved the light on Sam, who ran past the sasquatch and charged toward Gator Falls. His wings were open from wall to wall, their tips skimming the aquariums and startling the creatures inside.

Tameron and Hannah rushed after Sam, their unique powers revealed in Richie's shifting beam of light. Tameron was covered in animal armor, the spiked tip of his tail poised to strike. The bulging soles of Hannah's knee-high boots were now at least ten inches thick, and they sprang her forward five or six feet with each step.

As Hannah came upon the sasquatch, she pushed off the ground and spun high in the air like a gymnast. She kicked out her right foot and landed the sole of her boot on the chest of the sasquatch, which flew backward into the wall, shattering aquariums and spraying glass. The beast, unconscious or dead, lay in a web of busted metal framework, the contents of the aquariums spilling over its limp body. Spiders, cockroaches, centipedes, and beetles smacked the floor and scattered like beads of mercury. Hannah landed on her feet and continued forward, her stride unbroken.

"Richie!" Tameron said. "We need that light!"

Richie didn't move.

"Richie!" Tameron called again.

In the dim glow of the penlight, Noah saw Ella standing beside Richie. "Let's go," she said. "It's okay. I'm scared, too." They looked at each other for a moment, then turned and raced down the hall.

As Noah started to chase after them, someone grabbed his wrist. Unable to see without Richie's penlight, he turned to where he thought the person was standing. A voice said, "I'll catch up with you guys." It was Megan.

"Catch up? What are you—"

"We'll never do this without more light. These aquariums . . . they're all connected. If not through the Grottoes, then through the Secret Zoo."

"So?"

She released his wrist. "So I'm going to light this place up."

"What are you talking about?"

Staring at the darkness, Noah waited for an answer. When none came, he realized that she was gone.

"I hope you know what you're doing," he said to the empty air.

With that, Noah rushed down the hallway toward Gator Falls. He had no idea that he was about to face more danger than he had ever known.

❧ CHAPTER 35 ☙

TRAPPED

As Richie ran, the beam from his penlight slashed through the darkness, exposing random images: fake slime dripping from the ceiling; colorful frogs sticking to aquarium glass; rows of feathers shifting across Sam's wings; Tameron's tail sweeping along the floor.

The howl of a sasquatch shook the walls. An answering howl followed, then a third, then a chorus of deep, ape-like grunts. The noises echoed. Somewhere in front of Noah, Hannah shrieked for Sam. Then glass rained down on the hard floor.

The light swung around to reveal Sam falling backward

into Tameron and both of them dropping to the ground. Standing above them was a sasquatch. And another. And another.

Richie screamed and dropped the penlight, which pinged the floor and rolled to a stop, its beam pouring across a narrow stretch of tiles. An instant later, the light was kicked and sent sliding down the hall in a dizzying circle. It finally came to a stop beneath the foot of a sasquatch, which promptly crushed it, surrendering the hallway to pure darkness.

Noah halted. The ground felt slippery underfoot, and he realized he was standing on the tip of Sam's wing. He backed away until he could feel the tiles once more.

Silence. Noah had no idea what was happening. The darkness concealed all. It seemed a living thing, a bold new enemy as powerful and dangerous as the sasquatches.

Then the hallway filled with a new sound—the loud hiss of an alligator. It was nearby, perhaps only a few steps away. Noah heard the growl of a sasquatch and whirled around, straining to see something—anything. The monsters were prowling around the scouts and Descenders—their prey. They were preparing to strike.

Something bumped into Noah, and he spun in a panic. Darkness and fear magnified his confusion.

Sam's voice rose. "Descenders!"

Sam was somewhere near the center of the hallway, a few feet ahead.

Voices rose from different spots, one after another.

"Here," called Solana.

"Here," echoed Hannah.

"Right behind you," said Tameron.

The sasquatches growled.

"Anyone hurt?" Sam asked.

No one said yes.

"And the scouts? You guys okay?"

Everyone but Megan answered. Noah used their voices to determine their whereabouts. They all were nearby, but scattered.

Something swept along Noah's foot. He jumped away toward the middle of the hall, where the side of his lower leg pressed against something. Hearing a rolling growl, Noah realized he was standing against an alligator. Afraid to move again, he scanned the floor and tried again to see in the darkness—a wasted effort.

Across the hallway, Richie shrieked. Then he said, "Alligators—they're all over the place!"

A second alligator bumped Noah's leg—this time, his right. It quickly veered toward Noah, forcing his foot up along its body. Noah found himself standing on one leg, his toes skipping off the knobby surface of the alligator's back.

Sam called out, "Everyone—stay still!"

A third alligator struck the front of the leg Noah was standing on. It hissed. Then it gushed its warm breath over Noah's shin as it opened its mouth. Noah sensed its snout just inches from his knee, and he imagined the uneven rows of fangs hovering near his flesh.

Noah wobbled and tried to keep from falling. There was nowhere for him to go.

Across the dark hallway, Ella gasped. Richie whimpered. In horror, Noah understood that what was happening to him was happening to everyone. A crowd of alligators were squeezing themselves around the scouts. They were totally trapped.

CHAPTER 36

NEW LIGHT

Megan, having run down a different hallway, slowed when she sensed she was at its end. She threw her arms forward and touched the space around her. Her finger-tips soon found something soft and velvety—the curtain hanging above the entrance to the Chamber of Lights.

Big gold rings clattered along an overhead rod as she threw open the curtain. When she stepped into the room, which was no bigger than a walk-in closet, her memories of the day she'd vanished into the Dark Lands from this place sent a chill through her. In the exhibit's single wall-mounted aquarium, dozens of flashlight fish blinked on and off like underwater fireflies. She stepped up and placed her palms against the glowing glass.

"I . . . I don't know if you can understand me," she said softly. "Maybe you can, the way Blizzard and Podgy and Marlo seem to."

The fish continued to swim back and forth, winking on and off at random intervals. A few gathered near the front of the tank.

"We're in trouble. The sasquatches . . . they're escaping. The whole zoo is dark. I've seen what you can do, the way you can light up."

In her mind, Megan returned to the day she had disappeared from this very room—the start of her terrifying ordeal as a prisoner of the sasquatches. She remembered how the peculiar fish had begun to brightly glow until they pushed forward a blinding light, sending her to the Dark Lands.

She paused to collect her thoughts. "We need you to help us. We need your light across Creepy Critters. All the aquariums . . . they connect . . . we've learned that."

Her effort suddenly seemed pointless. Surely these fish couldn't understand her. Could they even hear her? Did her voice penetrate the glass?

One of the fish stopped blinking and began instead to steadily glow. The darkness lifted from Megan's hands, which were still pressed against the glass. Then it lifted from her arms, her chest. The walls of the Chamber of Lights slowly came into view.

A second fish began to shine, then a third, a fourth. As the darkness continued to melt away, Megan realized something was standing beside her. With a yelp, she turned and discovered Podgy. He'd apparently followed her down the hall.

"What are you . . ."

Podgy poked his head toward her and fluttered his eyelids. He then stepped forward and pinged his bill against the glass. Hearing the sound, the flashlight fish swarmed to the front of the tank, mere inches from the point of the penguin's bill. Podgy tapped the glass a few more times, then turned and waddled out of the room, the dim light of the fish following him.

Just outside the Chamber of Lights, Podgy faced the aquarium through the open door. Then he raised his flippers to the darkness around him. Seeing this, the fish swam to the back of their aquarium, where, one by one, they disappeared into a hollow branch. Within seconds, all of them had vanished toward the Secret Zoo, taking the light with them.

"No way . . ." Megan breathed. She wondered if this could possibly work.

She felt her way back out the door, where she bumped into Podgy. She stared down the hall that she'd just crossed, seeing nothing. Soon, however, points of light began to dot the darkness along the walls. Megan counted ten, fifteen, thirty. They illuminated the aquariums like tiny bulbs. The fish were portaling into different aquariums, just as Megan had hoped they would. She knew by their number that they were coming from the Secret Zoo.

The shape of the hallway began to appear—its height, its width, its jags and turns. Then, all at once, the spots began to shine more brightly as the fish spilled forth their magic light. It took only seconds for the tanks, the tiles, the fake goop and vines to become clear.

The normal habitants of the tanks that the flashlight fish had invaded were swimming circles in corners. In dry aquariums, snakes coiled along branches, spiders stuck to the back glass, and crabs pinched one another's claws.

As the flashlight fish continued to glow, Podgy waddled in front of Megan and turned his back to her. What he wanted was obvious, and Megan wrapped her arms around him, just below his neck.

"Let's go," she said.

Podgy raised his flippers, took a few strides, and lunged into flight. Megan nestled into position across his back, letting her legs dangle behind her the way she'd seen Noah do. Podgy soared down the hall, veering from side to side. As the corridor zigzagged, so did Podgy. He nearly bounced off the aquariums, startling fish behind strands of seaweed.

At the end of the hallway, Podgy swept into the Creepy Core and hung a right turn. Without hesitation, he flew toward Gator Falls, where the others were trapped.

CHAPTER 37

THE ADVANCE

Noah stood on his left leg while one alligator crept beneath his right foot and a second alligator waited in front of him, its mouth hinged open. He teetered, almost completely lost his balance, then righted himself again.

To his side rose a single point of light. It seemed to float in space, a pinch of brightness that reminded him of a glow-in-the-dark button. He strained to see where it was coming from and guessed a tank on the other side of the hall. Seconds after it appeared, so did another, this one roughly ten feet down from it. Then a third dot arose, and then a fourth. All down the hall, glowing spots pierced the darkness.

He turned back to his predicament with the alligators. Knowing he had to do something, he lowered his right leg, feeling the space with his toes to see if the alligator had passed. Finally, it had. He immediately dropped his foot to the newly vacant spot and swiveled away from the open mouth of the alligator, which snapped shut at that very moment.

As the bright spots continued to appear along the walls, Noah realized what they were: flashlight fish, the fish the scouts had encountered in the Chamber of Lights. They were using the Secret Zoo to swim into new aquariums. Noah had no doubt that his sister was responsible for this. Surely she wanted their magical light to illuminate the entire exhibit.

From somewhere beside Noah rose Ella's whimpering voice: "Guys . . . I'm in trouble." Her words were followed by a sasquatch's grunt and an alligator's growl. There was a thud against the floor—the footfall of a sasquatch. *"Big trouble!"*

The flashlight fish began to shine brighter, illuminating the tanks and the edges of the hallway. Noah swept his stare across the aquariums. Those that were filled with water had been invaded by flashlight fish. In the other tanks, the dry ones, snakes and lizards and giant millipedes raced along the glass, spooked by everything unfolding.

As more and more light poured forth, the entire hallway took shape. For the first time, Noah saw the floor—and it terrified him. In both directions, it was packed with alligators. They were crawling toward the Creepy Core, their bodies squirming above the thrusts of their stubby legs, their staggered fangs protruding from closed jaws.

Ella was standing beside one wall, and Richie the other. Surrounded by alligators, the two looked as if they were wading through a horrific river with reptilian spikes in the place of waves and whitecaps. To Noah, it looked like something from a nightmare.

Around the Descenders, the alligators bumped and jostled one another. Tameron's tail was buried among their bodies, and Sam's wings were raised high.

Sasquatches were scattered about. Standing with their knees bent and their arms raised, they looked ready to pounce. They inched through the crowd, their enormous feet rubbing against the alligators' bodies.

Sam's voice rang out. "Descenders—I'm counting twelve sasquatches! You seeing the same?"

In unison, his friends answered yes.

Noah stared past the Descenders and saw Gator Falls near the end of the hall, about forty yards away. Reaching from the floor to the ceiling, it looked like a swampy wetland covered in tall grass, moss, and lily pads. In it, two levels were joined by muddy inclines, and three waterfalls spilled from the higher level into a shallow pool. Alligators were crawling out of a broken glass wall. Because they were headed toward the Creepy Core, the short hallway section beyond the exhibit was empty.

Noah pointed down the hall. "See that clearing? We got to get over there!"

An alligator snapped at Ella, just missing her as she jumped to an open tile on the floor.

Richie said, "Whatever we do, we better do it soon!"

"Guys!" Hannah called. "Look!"

From out of the Creepy Core and into the hallway flew Podgy and Megan. As Podgy soared over the alligators, he dipped and rose and swerved, deliberately brushing the bulge of his stomach along their backs. The agitated reptiles snapped at him, missing by inches as he veered all around.

Sam said, "Tameron! Give me a path behind Podgy!"

"You got it."

Richie said, "What are—"

Sam cut him off. "Everyone! When Podgy flies by, fall in line behind me!"

"But you're surrounded by alligators!" Richie pointed out.

Sam cast a hard stare at Richie. "Not for long." He then

turned to Tameron, whose tail swept high into the air.

Richie's jaw dropped.

"Solana and Hannah—if the sasquatches come at us, stop them," Sam instructed.

Solana nodded. Hannah popped her gum.

As Podgy reached the sasquatches, he steered through them, keeping just beyond the swing of their arms. Alligators continued to snap at him, their front legs springing from the floor. Podgy's flippers smacked their broad snouts, almost insultingly.

As soon as Podgy soared past, Tameron jumped in front of Sam and spun his tail around, sweeping the alligators aside. Like snow behind the push of a plow, the alligators flew through the air. When the tail reached Sam, he jumped it like a rope, allowing the floor around him to be cleared.

Noah looked on in disbelief. Tameron had opened a circle on the floor that spanned the width of the hallway. Alligators lay against the walls, heaped atop one another, writhing and kicking and biting. Their tails snapped and thrashed, smashing out the fronts of aquariums and filling the hallway with the sharp reports of shattering glass.

"Move!" Sam ordered.

Hannah pushed off on the soles of her boots and sprang into the air toward the open circle. She grabbed the wrists of Solana's raised arms and pulled her along. The girls dropped into the clearing and rolled gracefully to their feet.

Five or six alligators separated Noah from the clearing where the Descenders now stood. Ella and Richie were in the same predicament, and both were looking at Noah for direction. Knowing they didn't have time to waste, Noah began jumping across the alligators' backs, his ankles rolling on their knobby spikes. Each time he pushed off one, it whipped around, snapping at the space he'd just emptied. Ella and Richie followed his lead, and it took only seconds for the three of them to reach the open circle.

With everyone in position, Sam called out, "Tameron—go!"

Tameron ran to the edge of the clearing, where he crouched and again swung his tail around, beginning a fresh sweep of the crowded floor. Once more, the alligators went airborne and crashed into the walls, shattering glass and spilling the contents of aquariums—black beetles and spiny-legged spiders.

As Tameron worked, so did Sam. He reached his wings out to his sides so that a wall of feathers rose from the center of the circle to stretch the width of the hall. Startled at the sight, many alligators retreated, crawling over one another, hissing and growling and biting. As Sam advanced toward Gator Falls, the scouts,

Hannah, and Solana stayed huddled behind him.

The sasquatches stood by and watched. One beat its knuckles against its chest. Another punched its fist into a fish tank, which spilled like a waterfall onto the alligators beneath it.

"Okay . . ." Ella said. "Those guys look really, really mad."

A sasquatch charged across the alligators and leaped into the clearing. Hannah sprang forward and flipped over, landing briefly on a handstand before thrusting the soles of her boots squarely against the sasquatch's gut. The monster buckled over and flew through the air. Far down the hall, it crashed to the ground and slid on the tiles, bumping alligators out of its path before finally coming to a stop near the Creepy Core in a heap of muscle and mangy hair.

Ella turned to Richie. "And you always thought *your* shoes were pretty cool."

When a second sasquatch lunged into the open space, Solana threw her shoulder forward and sank dozens of quills into its body. Rubbing its chest, the beast staggered back to the edge of the clearing and stumbled over the alligators. As it hit the tiles, the confused reptiles attacked it, their powerful jaws clamping onto its body.

Tameron continued to swing his tail around, opening a path for the other Crossers. Sam stroked his arms up and down, sending waves through his wings and frightening the alligators back.

"Guys!" Sam momentarily dropped his wings. "Look!"

The sasquatches ahead of them were retreating into Gator Falls, fleeing back into the Secret Zoo.

A minute later, Tameron pushed the last of the alligators aside, and the group moved into the open area at the end of the hall, where Megan and Podgy were waiting. In front of Gator Falls, glass lay everywhere, glinting in the shine of the flashlight fish. Looking into the exhibit was like peering into a swamp full of rich, deep greens. From the middle waterfall, a trail of alligators was still emerging.

"That middle waterfall . . ." said Sam. "Beyond it is a straight drop to the Secret Creepy Critters. We got to get in there and close the portal. The curtain . . . it has to come down. It'll seal off the sector immediately."

"How do we get past the alligators?" Richie asked.

"The tunnel beyond the waterfall is at least ten feet high. We have to go in through the top."

Understanding what Sam was getting at, they all turned to Podgy, who merely returned their gazes in his usual ho-hum manner.

Noah stepped in beside the emperor penguin, saying, "I'll go with him. Someone has to pull off the curtain." When the other scouts protested, Noah immediately raised his hand, saying, "There's no time to talk about this."

"The two of them fly best together," Sam pointed out.

Noah moved in behind Podgy and draped his arms over his body, just above his flippers. "This is the only way."

Sam told him, "The curtain—it's not going to come down easy. But pull hard enough, and it will."

Noah nodded.

"The Secret Creepy Critters looks a lot like this place"—Sam gestured to the fake gunk dripping from the ceiling and the walls of aquariums around him—"only bigger—*much* bigger. You'll portal into the Secret Gator Falls. Find an open spot to swing around in. As soon as you pass back through the portal, grab the curtain and don't let go."

"You got that, Podge?" Noah asked.

Podgy cocked his head to one side in what seemed like a yes.

"Noah, get in and out of the Secret Creepy Critters as fast as you can. It's not . . ." Sam's voice trailed off. He chose his next words carefully. "It's not a place you want to be."

☙ CHAPTER 38 ❧

THE SECRET CREEPY CRITTERS

To build up speed, Podgy and Noah flew down the hallway into the Creepy Core and circled back. On their return, they veered into Gator Falls through the broken wall of glass and steered toward the middle waterfall. They struck the falls and passed into the tunnel, Noah's head missing the ceiling by at least a foot.

Sloping down into the ground, the tunnel was at least fifty yards long. Its brick walls glistened with moisture from the falls, and water streamed down the tiny mortar trenches onto the dirt floor, muddying it. The wet tunnel ended at a single velvet curtain. Alligators were steadily crawling out from under it, juggling the muddy tassels along their backs.

As Podgy flew along the top of the cave, his flippers reached above Noah and clapped against the ceiling. He sped along, leaving little time for the alligators to do more than lift their snouts and hiss. A few snapped at the space beneath him.

When Podgy came to the portal, he flattened his flippers against his sides and pushed his bill forward, streamlining his body. Noah turned his head and squeezed his eyes shut. They hit the curtain and were filled with Bhanu's magic. As they portaled into the Secret Gator Falls, Noah opened his eyes and felt his heart jump.

The Secret Gator Falls looked like the zoo exhibit it was attached to. Steep, grassy inclines rose all around, and countless waterfalls fell from the heights. Alligators crowded the ground, their feet splashing through mud, their bodies streaming along the surface of shallow streams.

Noah sensed something behind him and peered over his shoulder. Five sasquatches were chasing after them, each heaving its weight across all four of its limbs, like an ape.

"Podgy!" Noah called out. "Behind us!"

Just as Noah looked forward again, Podgy swerved to miss a waterfall and flew in behind it. They moved beside the wall of water like a surfboarder beside the falling crest of a wave. Noah squinted against a cloud of mist, and a second later, the duo emerged in the open air again, Noah blinking the water out of his eyes.

An alligator sprang forward into the air and snapped its jaws at Noah's feet, just missing. A second alligator attacked, and then a third. Noah swung his dangling legs left and right to avoid their bites. Podgy flew beneath another waterfall, this time soaking Noah, whose wet earflaps clung to the sides of his head.

Seconds later, they came upon the long stretch of a wall of water. Unable to go around it, Podgy went through it, and he and Noah appeared in a new space. Here, there were no alligators. Thick fog hung all around, and moss-covered branches reached out at them like the grabbing arms of monsters. The ground was muddied, pitted with holes, and marked with patches of thin grass, their long blades drooping under the weight of the air. Bugs were everywhere, running across everything. There was still no place big enough to turn around.

Podgy twisted his head back for a brief look and continued forward. As they flew between two tall bushes, something that felt like thread struck Noah's face. It clung to his cheeks and invaded his mouth. He swiped one hand over his lips, and the thin material stuck to his fingers. Podgy, he realized, had just flown through a massive cobweb. Spiders were crawling all over them. There were hundreds, their bodies round as marbles, their legs thick as toothpicks.

Noah swiped at his arm again and again. Spiders flew into the air and burst beneath his palms, their gooey guts smearing his jacket. Noah lost his hold and slid down the penguin's side, flattening his flipper. With only one working wing, Podgy veered into the ground, spraying mud everywhere. When Noah fell off his back and rolled, something spilled over him. He lay in darkness, covered in something—something that was moving. He felt thousands of tiny legs pattering along his body, pricking his clothes and skin.

Noah pushed himself to his hands and knees, slinging the unknown things everywhere. He stared out. All around him, the ground was . . . *writhing*. What looked like snakes, Noah realized, were centipedes—giant centipedes, each nearly a foot long. They crawled over his body, their segmented bodies squirming. When Noah felt one on his bare neck, he pinched it in his fingertips and flung it into the air, where it twirled away end over end.

Overcome with revulsion, he jumped to his feet, centipedes tumbling off his body. He felt them moving inside his jacket and frantically unzipped it and flung it to the ground, where the swell of centipedes absorbed it.

Behind him came a low, angry growl. Noah swung

around and saw nothing but fog. In front of him, a new growl echoed the first. He spun back, centipedes popping beneath his feet. Again nothing. Only fog. Then growls came from new places. He turned and turned. Nothing. He waited. The only sound was the dull clinking of the centipedes' hard bodies, the soft patter of their steps.

On all sides of Noah, the fog began to churn and break apart. One after another, sasquatches began to appear. They prowled toward Noah, crunching centipedes.

Noah searched for his penguin friend. "Podgy! Over here!"

The sasquatches crept forward, their beastly forms rising out of the fog.

Centipedes continued to squirm up Noah's legs. Heaps crawled beyond his waist, blanketing his body with theirs. Several slipped beneath his shirt and writhed along his skin. One wormed up to his shoulder, and Noah felt a pinpoint of pain as he was bitten. He reached under his collar, grabbed the centipede, and chucked it away.

"Podddggyyy!"

The sasquatches closed in. Centipedes were crawling all over them, burrowing through their long hair. A sasquatch howled and batted one off its arm. Another reached over its shoulder, pulled away a centipede, then chomped off its head and tossed its gooey remains aside.

Noah's insides churned. He cupped his hands around his mouth: *"Pooodddgggyyyy!"*

The emperor penguin burst forward, his flippers stirring the fog. He swerved around a sasquatch, narrowly eluding the swipe of its claws, and headed for Noah, flying low. Noah grabbed hold of the penguin and slung himself onto his back. His sudden weight plunged Podgy into the centipedes, but the penguin veered back into the air, his flippers flinging the arthropods all around. He steered through two other sasquatches and headed back to the portal to the Clarksville Zoo.

Noah said, "I can't believe that worked!"

As they flew back through the wide waterfall, Podgy gained more and more speed. The curtain appeared. Dangling from a rod, it covered an opening along a steep, muddy slope. Beneath it, alligators crawled; around it, four sasquatches stood guard. As Podgy approached, the sasquatches fixed their eyes on him.

"They see us!"

Less than a hundred feet from the curtain now, Podgy flew at a breathtaking pace, veering from side to side as he negotiated the best angle of approach. Noah hung on, his legs fishtailing in the air behind him. They reached the sasquatches, and the first one swung at Podgy, who dodged the blow. The big penguin dipped and swerved through the attacks of the others, then pushed through the portal. As the curtain brushed against Noah, he pinched it in the crook of his arm and pulled with all his might. One after another, the gold rings snapped free from the overhead rod—*clink! clink! clink! clink!*—sounding like machine-gun fire in an old video game.

As Noah listened for the last ring to break apart, it didn't, and he was yanked into the air. He swung backward on the curtain, watching in horror as Podgy flew deeper into the Clarksville Zoo without him.

In front of Noah, an alligator turned back its long snout and spotted him. Then it whipped its body around and pried open its jaws, ready to strike.

CHAPTER 39

ANYTHING BOYS CAN DO . . .

As soon as Noah and Podgy disappeared through the waterfall toward the Secret Creepy Critters, Sam turned to the other Crossers and said, "The alligators—we have to stop them." He became distracted in his own thoughts, then touched his ear, saying, "Charlie? You out there? We're still waiting for backup!" He waited for a response, his eyes shifting over random spots. "Charlie, I repeat! We're—"

Sam's body lurched forward, his winged arms sailing out beside him. He clunked his head on the ground and lay perfectly still, his limp wings spread like a blanket across his back.

"Sam!" Solana cried.

For a second, Ella didn't understand what had happened. Then she saw a sasquatch where Sam had been standing. It had knocked him down, the blow leaving him unconscious.

The sasquatches from down the hall were advancing on them, seeming to wade upstream in a nightmarish river of alligators. One reached the clearing and attacked Tameron, seizing his tail and yanking him off his feet. In an explosion of glass, the Descender slammed into one wall of aquariums. He dropped to the floor and lay perfectly still, bugs raining down on him like horrific confetti.

Into the clearing stepped the other sasquatches, one after another. At the edge of the alligators, they stood with their arms raised to their sides. One threw itself forward and struck its palms against Richie's chest, hurling him backward. Richie thudded onto the floor and rolled to a stop at the end of the hallway against the outside wall, clutching his chest in pain.

"Richie!" Ella screamed.

As the four girls quickly came together in the middle of the open space, the sasquatches slunk along the walls, surrounding them.

Megan said, "What do we do?"

"The only thing we can do," Hannah answered. She

popped a small bubble, then crouched low. "We fight until it's done."

The Descender sprang forward and spun high in the air, kicking out her leg and the powerful weapon of her boot. When she connected with a sasquatch, it buckled sideways, flew into the wall of aquariums, and dropped to its knees in a shower of glass. Two others attacked, one on each side. Hannah crouched low and swept around her leg in a roundhouse kick, taking out their feet. Another dove at her, and she jumped all the way to the ceiling, her legs brought up in a spread-eagled stretch so that the beast stumbled beneath her. On her way down, she kicked one leg back, planting it squarely against the monster's rump and sending it headfirst into the wall.

A sasquatch came up behind Hannah, seized her shoulders, and held her in the air away from its body. Hannah kicked back but couldn't connect. Another sasquatch moved in, its claws pulled back to strike. Before it could, Megan and Ella jumped onto its arm, and the monster staggered and dropped to the floor.

Solana jumped in behind the sasquatch that was holding Hannah. She reached across her body and tore a handful of quills from her side. Then she swung her arm around and pitched the quills into the sasquatch's back. The beast arched its shoulders, releasing Hannah.

Ella stood there, stunned. Prying her eyes from Solana,

she looked around. Sasquatches were lying all over, some unconscious, others dazed. Somehow, the girls were winning.

Ella suddenly remembered Richie and turned toward the end of the hall. She shuddered. Richie was still lying on the ground. And two sasquatches were moving in on him.

◆⊙ CHAPTER 40 ⊙◆

RUMBLES IN THE WALL

Propped up on his elbows, Richie watched helplessly as the sasquatches neared. In the outside wall behind him, the aquariums suddenly shook. He craned his neck back to see water sloshing and fish darting nervously about.

The wall shook a second time. A third. Water spilled out the tops of the aquariums and cascaded down the glass. The fish swam out of sight and escaped toward the Secret Zoo. The two sasquatches raised their eyes at the commotion. One snorted, spraying snot.

The wall rocked again. And again. Richie watched as

cracks formed in the glass—cracks that quickly spread and joined together.

"Uh-oh," Richie said.

Just as he wrapped his head in his arms, the right side of the shaking wall imploded, and the hall filled with pieces of glass and metal and brick, the debris streaming past him. Water spilled everywhere. Through a cloud of dust lunged two animals that Richie knew. Blizzard and Little Bighorn.

As the rhino landed, his big hooves shattered the tiles. He turned, and with a sideways jerk of his head, scooped up one sasquatch and heaved it up to the ceiling. The monster crashed into the fake goop and then dropped to the floor, unmoving.

Blizzard rammed into the other sasquatch, sank his teeth into its ankle, and slung it against the wall with a pull of his long neck. The monster dropped to the ground. When it tried to raise itself, it immediately collapsed, pieces of glass showering across its back.

Through a gaping hole in the wall, Tank appeared. He kicked through the wreckage and hoisted Richie to his feet. Then he reached out and straightened Richie's glasses. "Sorry we're late, bub."

"Huh?" said a dazed Richie.

"We're late. Sorry about that. I had to round up a crew."

Richie had no idea what he was talking about. Richie, in

fact, had no real concept of much at the moment. "Crew?"

Tank glanced out the broken wall into the dark night. "Here they come now."

Richie peered outside. Nothing was there.

"Don't sweat it. They're just birds. And you've met them before." He suddenly laid a hand on Richie's head, palming it like a basketball. "But you're going to want to duck for this."

As the big man dropped, pulling Richie along, birds poured in from the open wall, an endless number, of black-capped chickadees. Their wings a fluttery blur, they filled the top half of the hallway, their sheer numbers blotting out the ceiling. Loose feathers rained down, a few of them landing on Tank's bald head, looking startlingly white against his dark skin. The chickadees swarmed past the girls, who'd dropped to their hands and knees.

In groups of a hundred or more, some birds carried large nets in their tiny talons. Seconds after flying into the building, one group dropped its net on a sasquatch, which thrashed its arms, entangled itself, and fell to the ground. The same pack of chickadess then swooped down and drew in the edges of the net, bundling and twisting their captive, leaving it snarling and biting at the cords.

A second group of chickadees released their net over another sasquatch and repeated the same process. Within seconds, the beast was left growling and writhing on the floor.

Richie looked again at the girls. Covered in chickadee feathers, Ella and Megan were sitting on their knees, cheering. Solana was leaning forward with her forehead pressed against the floor, as if in thankful prayer. Hannah burst a bubble against a broad smile.

The chickadees continued to stream in through the open wall. Down the length of the hall, flashlight fish revealed the action: birds swarming, nets dropping, sasquatches being caught.

As Richie and Tank watched, Tank asked, "Ever dream you'd see chickadees catching something as big and ugly as a sasquatch?"

Richie met his friend's stare. "Nuh-uh. No way."

"Well, that's how we roll, bub." Tank smiled. "That's how we roll in the Secret Zoo."

Richie thought about this. "That's great. But next time, you think you could roll a little more quickly?"

The big man bellowed with laughter and swatted Richie's shoulder, nearly knocking him down.

Richie straightened and looked around. Things weren't over, not yet. Alligators were still escaping. And the gateway to the Secret Creepy Critters needed to be closed.

Thinking of the latter, Richie peered over at the middle waterfall in Gator Falls. There was still no sign of Noah or Podgy.

CHAPTER 41

A Pendulum Between Two Worlds

Noah, his hands clutching the curtain, swung back into the Secret Creepy Critters, the world blurring on both of his sides. At his rearward peak, a sasquatch swiped at him, but its claws whooshed over Noah's head as he dropped back down. The curtain's tassels pulled through the mud, and Noah portaled again in Gator Falls. He swung out and up, then slowed to a stop in the air. An alligator lunged at him, its jaws snapping shut on emptiness just as Noah was pulled back toward the sector. The curtain had become a pendulum between two worlds.

As he passed beneath the rod, he peered up. A single ring was all that held the curtain.

For Noah, the cave again became the sector. As the curtain swung out, a sasquatch moved in front of the portal, a snarl on its face. Having to think fast, Noah kicked his legs forward as he came down, crashing his feet against the monster and sending it with him back into Gator Falls.

In the tunnel, several alligators had turned back. The sasquatch stepped on the snout of one and fell to the ground. As the confused alligator sprang open its jaws, Noah spread-eagled his legs to avoid its bite. The curtain lifted him high, then down again. As he fell, he bounced his heels on the reptile's snout, driving it into the mud.

Noah couldn't keep this up. The curtain had to come down. But it needed to happen while he was in Gator Falls. If it didn't, he'd be trapped in the Secret Zoo.

He portaled out of the Clarksville Zoo again and up into the air. As the curtain dropped from its highest reach, he peered over his shoulder and saw a sasquatch charging on all fours. Noah heaved his weight forward and passed across the magical threshold in front of the reaching arms of the sasquatch. As he swung upward in the tunnel, the alligator that he'd just kicked into the mud poked up its snout, only to land it in the clutches of the sasquatch, which seemed to confuse it for Noah.

Seeing his chance, Noah pulled against the velvet folds with all his might. The final ring snapped, the curtain fell, and Noah splashed into the mud. He stared back at where the portal had been and saw a solid wall. In it, the sasquatch's arms were trapped, its powerful hands clenching the snout of the alligator, which was thrashing from side to side, trying to free itself.

In the corners of his eyes, Noah saw something move. A sasquatch—the one that he'd kicked through the gateway. On its hands and knees, it shook the confusion out of its head, then lifted its gaze. Spotting Noah, it dropped its eyebrows, then slammed its boulderlike fists against the ground. It howled, sending thin streams of spit into the air.

A loud hiss sounded behind Noah. He jerked around and stared directly into two nostrils. The dark holes lifted as an alligator spread its jaws, revealing crooked fangs and a bulging tongue. Noah threw himself aside and tried to get away. But this time, there was no narrow escape. This time, the alligator clamped down on Noah, sinking its sharp teeth into his body.

✦ CHAPTER 42 ✦

P-Dog Sets the Trap

P-Dog poked his head up from the secret tunnel beside Little Dogs of the Prairie. He glanced in every direction, then leaped out with a squeaky grunt. He turned back, rose onto his haunches, and yipped once. From the tunnel emerged his companions, one after another, more than a hundred trampling onto the snowy lawn of the Clarksville Zoo. P-Dog charged off, leading the prairie dogs toward their destination—Creepy Critters.

At the exhibit, the animals bounded up the staircase to the front entrance, stepping around shards of glass and metal. P-Dog gave the air an investigative sniff and moved inside. Alligators covered the floor as they crawled for the open doorway, their fangs gleaming in the hall's magic light.

P-Dog swung his head back and yipped wildly. The prairie dogs, massed together, stormed into the building. Growling and hissing, the alligators parted their jaws and prepared to strike.

When the two groups collided, P-Dog slipped into the open mouth of an alligator. As it chomped down, he sprang off its spongy tongue and landed on the back of a second alligator. By the time this one swung around to attack, P-Dog had already jumped to the back of a third. Then he cleared the space to a fourth, a fifth, crossing their knobby backs like stepping-stones.

Yipping and squealing, the other prairie dogs scampered across the alligators, crossing their tails and backs like the rugged terrain of a familiar savanna. The alligators thrashed and bucked and bit, their jaws closing far behind the rodents' rumps. As one prairie dog reached an about-facing alligator, he ran across its back and leaped from its inclined snout as if from a diving board.

The flashlight fish continued to shine. Darkness seemed huddled in corners, fearful of their magic.

As P-Dog veered into the Creepy Core, he came upon the open jaws of three alligators, all in a row. He darted through them, hurdling their teeth. The mouths snapped shut one after another, missing him each time.

P-Dog led the prairie dogs down the hall toward Gator Falls. The alligators continued to turn back to chase them, having no idea they were heading into a trap.

Richie pointed down the hallway beneath the chickadees and rolled his head toward Tank, saying, "Is that . . . is that P-Dog?"

Tank roared laughter. "Yep."

"But won't he . . . like . . . get eaten?"

"Not if he's fast."

Richie watched a new group of chickadees release their net—this time, over a grouping of alligators. The alligators thrashed about, entangling themselves. Unable to move, they simply lay there, their legs meshed in the rope. The chickadees then descended and dragged the edges of the net forward, scooping it around their captives and pulling it tight.

Prairie dogs leaped out of the way as another wave of chickadees dropped a second net. Then came a third net, a fourth, a fifth, like bombs from airplanes. More and more alligators become snarled, twisted, and trapped.

It took only minutes for the alligators in the hall to be contained. The chickadees then went to work on the ones escaping from the tunnel to the Secret Zoo.

Ella called out, "Guys—look!" She pointed toward Gator Falls, where Podgy had just punched through the middle waterfall. One thing stopped Richie from feeling good about this.

Noah wasn't on his back.

⊰ CHAPTER 43 ⊱

COLLATERAL MAGIC

Noah was picked up by the alligator and whipped from side to side. He felt its tongue shift and roll and heat radiate from its throat.

He realized something. Though his torso was being squeezed, he couldn't feel any pain. He glanced down and saw he was wrapped in the curtain. After stripping it from the rod, he'd become entangled in it. Now, somehow, its magic was protecting him from being mauled to pieces.

The alligator knew nothing of this. It continued to thrash Noah about, trying to snap his spine. One of the alligator's dark eyes was inches from Noah's face. The size of a golf ball, it blinked once . . . twice. It was watching Noah, waiting to see the life escape him.

Beside them, the sasquatch swiped mud from its eyes and growled. It prowled toward Noah, ready to strike. As the alligator snapped its head around, Noah swept his legs beneath the sasquatch's feet, dropping it back to the ground.

Knowing he had to do something, Noah threw a desperate punch against the alligator's fleshy throat. Its jaws opened, and Noah fell to the ground and rolled aside, shedding the curtain in the process. He jumped to his feet, and the alligator lurched forward and snapped at him, just missing.

Noah sidestepped so the alligator stood between him and the sasquatch. The sasquatch climbed to one knee, its back turned to Noah.

Noah saw an opportunity. He snatched up the curtain in one hand and ran across the alligator's back. He pitched his arm around, and the curtain opened like a parachute and touched down on the sasquatch, covering its top half. Then he jumped onto the monster's back and coiled his arms around its neck, cinching the velvet cloth over its head.

The sasquatch lurched forward, blind and confused. It smashed against the wall, crumbling bricks. Noah stared up the tunnel. Close to two hundred feet ahead, he saw the end of it—a point of light shimmering in the waterfall. As many as fifteen alligators separated him from the exit.

Noah cupped his mouth around the monster's ear. *"Grraaaahhhhh!"*

The sasquatch spun around, trying to pinpoint the source of the noise.

"Graaa-OOOHHH!"

The sasquatch, still crouched, took off running up the tunnel, feeling its way with outstretched arms. It banged against the walls and splashed mud up the bricks. It stepped on alligators, driving their snouts and stomachs to the ground. Noah held on and bounced about, his world blurring back and forth.

"Rrraaaggghh! Erraahhhh! Ahhh!"

The spot of light grew bigger and brighter. The vague spill of the waterfall became beaded streams. Hissing alligators snapped at the sasquatch's feet, some diving against the walls to avoid being trampled.

"Naarrrggghhh!"

Through the wavering lens of the waterfall, Noah began to make out the shapes of people. Tank and Blizzard and Little Bighorn. Somehow they'd been pulled into the melee. Above them flew a mass of tiny round birds. Chickadees.

The sasquatch burst through the wall of water and carried Noah into the exhibit. It splashed through the shallow pool, then staggered into the hallway. Noah let go and thudded onto his back. He blinked his eyes dry and saw the sasquatch throw off the velvet curtain, only to be covered again, this time with a net.

Feathers rained down on him. Their slow, slicing movements reminded him of leaves falling in the City of Species. The other scouts rushed over and dropped to their knees beside him.

"Noah!" Megan said. "Are you okay?"

Too exhausted for words, Noah nodded.

"The curtain—you got it!"

"It's done." Noah stared into the eyes of his friends. "It's over."

The scouts collapsed across Noah, their arms draped over one another in a collective embrace.

The chickadees netted the few remaining alligators, then flew down the hall. Tank walked over to Hannah and Solana; together they watched the four friends hold one another.

"That's what gives them their strength," Tank said. "What you're looking at right there is what makes them the scouts."

A voice spoke behind them. "He's absolutely right."

The three Crossers turned to see Mr. Darby. He'd

stepped in from the hole in the wall and now stood beside them, his purple trench coat flowing onto the ground. Chickadees were perched along his velvet shoulders.

Mr. Darby touched Tank's shoulder. "Their strength has its source in their love. And we'll need that strength in our battles, I assure you."

Tank looked at the old man. He said nothing.

"Have no doubt. Their power is unique. If victory is ours to be had, it will be their love that helps deliver it."

Tank remained silent.

"Just wait," Mr. Darby added with a smile. "One day, Mr. Pangbourne, you will see. One day, you will see."

❧ CHAPTER 44 ❧

THE CLEANUP AND THE COVER-UP

$\mathcal{S}$am and Tameron were revived, and work began to clean up the mess. The chickadees left through the broken wall, headed toward the Forest of Flight and its hidden portal to the Secret Zoo. P-Dog led his coterie back to their exhibit. Mr. Darby informed everyone that order had been restored in the City of Species, the sasquatches having fled back into random sectors. There had been damage to the city, but no word yet on casualties.

Tank nodded. "I'll call Red . . . have him check on the lights." He touched his earpiece and said, "Charlie, it's Tank. Can you get ready with the lights? I don't know

how much longer these flashlight fish can do their thing."
He paused for Charlie's response, then added, "Roger.
We'll let you know when to throw the switch."

Tank turned back to the group—Mr. Darby, the scouts,
the Descenders, Blizzard, Podgy, and Little Bighorn. He
pointed down the hall to where alligators and sasquatches
wriggled in nets. "What do we do with them?"

Ella said, "The apes. From Metr-APE-olis. They're strong
and coordinated—trust me, I know. Maybe the apes could
take them back to the Secret Zoo through Giraffic Jam.
That exhibit's just around the corner. You guys must have
a big truck, right? Have the apes load them into a truck
and then someone drive them over to Giraffic Jam."

A smile stole across Mr. Darby's face. The old man
turned to the Descenders and said, "You see . . . already
they're thinking like Crossers."

Sam acknowledged this with a nod.

"I'll pull the apes," Tank said. "On my way back, I'll pick
up some wheels. And we'll need some Constructors, too."

Though Noah had no idea what a Constructor was,
apparently Mr. Darby did. The old man nodded. "Your
walkie-talkie, Mr. Pangbourne. I'll call Mr. Gordon on
the south perimeter and have him gather a crew."

Noah couldn't believe how prepared the Secret Society
was.

Tank unclipped his walkie-talkie and let it fly. Before it

landed in Mr. Darby's hands, he turned and headed for Metr-APE-olis.

Mr. Darby snagged the walkie-talkie out of the air and pressed its button. "Mr. Gordon? Mr. Gordon, are you there?"

A staticky voice arose from the speaker: "Gordon here."

"Mr. Gordon, we need the services of Constructors at Creepy Critters. Can you work on gathering a crew?"

"Roger that. When do you need them?"

"As soon as possible."

"Got it. Give me ten minutes."

A small burst of static sounded, and Mr. Gordon was gone.

"What are Constructors?" Ella asked.

Mr. Darby peered down the hall. "Ohhh . . . they fix things."

For a while, there was nothing to do but wait. At one point, Marlo appeared from nowhere and touched down on Noah's shoulder. At another, Blizzard padded up to the scouts and lovingly nudged Noah with his big head. Noah smiled and leaned into the bear, half disappearing into his deep white fur. Richie and Ella stood on either side of Little Bighorn, patting him. Megan waited beside Podgy.

After ten minutes had passed, Tank came through the busted wall leading a group of apes, as many as twenty. The apes grunted and snorted and sniffed the air with upturned nostrils. A large truck backed its semitrailer up against the building. In a cloud of exhaust, Tank jumped to the bumper and kicked a latch, opening the big rear door. He pulled out the loading ramp and dropped one end to the ground.

"Okay," Tank said. "Let's do this."

The apes went to work. They moved in groups on the alligators, not-so-gently dragging the nets across the floor and up the ramp. The scouts stood back and watched. The Descenders gathered the smaller animals that had got out—crabs and snakes and frogs and turtles—and returned them to their tanks, where they promptly escaped into the hidden passages leading to the Secret Zoo. The Descenders even collected the bugs they could find—beetles and spiders and anything else.

As the groups worked, four men with huge backpacks walked up behind Mr. Darby. To get his attention, one man said, "Nice mess—who made it?"

Mr. Darby spun around and smiled. "I'm not certain whom to blame, but I trust you can clean it up."

The men scanned the area. Noah realized they were the Constructors Mr. Darby had referred to.

"How much time we got?"

"Can you beat the sun?" Mr. Darby asked.

"Shouldn't be a problem. Most of the damage is superficial."

Noah scanned the surroundings: the shattered

aquariums, the mounds of debris, the busted tiles. He turned to Richie and mouthed, *Superficial?*

Richie shrugged. Apparently the damage didn't seem superficial to him, either.

The Constructors walked down the hall and opened a door marked "Employees Only." They wheeled out a flat-bed cart with a stack of thick glass panes. They pulled it down the hall and stopped at a spot that held the remains of at least ten busted aquariums. They slipped off their backpacks and rummaged through the contents.

To the scouts, Tank said, "Watch this."

One man worked a pry bar to reshape the twisted frame-work of an aquarium. Another man used a sharp-bladed tool to clean the edges. A third man then lifted a plate of glass to the place they were working, and the fourth man wiped a velvet towel across it. The magic moved a rect-angular piece of the pane into the face of the aquarium.

"Unbelievable . . ." Megan muttered.

"What's up with the velvet?" Ella asked Mr. Darby. "You grow it on a magic farm or something?"

"Patience," said Mr. Darby. "You will learn about it in your crosstraining. And ultimately . . . ultimately, you will see."

The Constructors proceeded to a second aquarium, then a third, a fourth, a fifth, each man performing a different task. Once they'd restored a full section of the wall, they hoisted their gear and wheeled the cart to a new area.

The apes continued to gather the animals, and a half hour later the truck was loaded. The floor of Creepy Critters looked strange in its new emptiness. Everyone congregated at the rear of the truck, and Tank pulled the trailer door closed.

"Okay," he said. "Me and the apes . . . we'll take care of biz from here."

Richie stepped forward. "Thanks, Tank. Thanks for being there again."

"No problem, little man." Tank extended his knuckles to Richie. "Give me one of these."

Richie softly punched his small fist against Tank's huge one. Then, with a smile, he shook out his hand and mouthed, *Owww!*

To the other scouts, Tank said, "And you guys?"

The three friends stepped forward and took turns tapping their fists against Tank's.

"That's what I'm talking about." Tank winked. To the Descenders, he said, "I'll see you guys back inside." He turned and whistled at the driver. The truck pulled out, spewing a final cloud of smoke into Creepy Critters. Tank led the apes across the yard, where they walked along the slow-moving vehicle. As it turned, moonlight struck its side and revealed what was written across it in bold letters: "DANGER! LIVE ANIMALS!"

Richie said, "I bet that sign has never been more true."

"I think not," Mr. Darby said with a smile. "And on

that note, I also think it's time for our scouts to return home before someone's found missing from bed."

"Yeah," said Noah. "I should probably close my window before my parents wake up and wonder where the draft is coming from."

Sam walked over to Noah. He started to say something and stopped. His eyes shifted nervously. At last, he said, "That was good. In the tunnel, with the curtain . . ." His mouth hung open while he searched for more words. "Just know you did good."

Noah's heart warmed. It was the first time a Descender had congratulated him on anything.

Hannah and Solana stepped up to Megan and Ella. Hannah said, "Nice job with that sasquatch. If you hadn't jumped on that thing . . ."

"Not a problem," Ella said. "We girls have to look out for each other, right?"

Hannah winked and popped a bubble.

With their good-byes complete, Mr. Darby said, "Blizzard and Little Bighorn, will the two of you kindly see that the scouts get safely to the front gates? We'll have Charlie keep the lights down until you return."

The two animals lumbered over, and the scouts climbed onto their backs, the boys on Blizzard and the girls on Little Bighorn. As Noah situated himself in his normal front seat, he looked down at Podgy.

"Podge, I have to be honest. Those centipedes not only grossed me out, they scared me to death."

Podgy tipped his bill beneath one flipper, a gesture of agreement.

"Centipedes?" Richie asked. "What are you—" His face shifted. "Hey! Speaking of centipedes . . . I got a really good joke!"

"What?" Noah gasped.

"A joke . . . I got a joke about centipedes!"

Ella shot Richie a look. "If you even *think* of telling one of your dumb jokes right now . . ."

"What?" Richie said. "You want me to save it for later?"

Noah laughed and tapped the side of Blizzard's neck. "C'mon, Bliz, let's get out of here."

Blizzard growled. Together, the two animals charged down the hall in the magical glow of the flashlight fish. They reached the Creepy Core and headed on to the exit. They barreled through the busted doors and jumped down to the ground. Side by side, they stormed through the darkness, their paws and hooves stamping impressions into the snow.

The scouts leaned forward and felt the cold breeze. Adrenaline coursed through them as another Secret Zoo adventure came to an end. As they neared the front gates, Noah raised his fist and cheered.

The other scouts followed his lead.

CHAPTER 45

THE TWO MEN

While the scouts made their way to the front gates, two men stepped into Rhinorama. Because the lights hadn't yet been restored, everything was perfectly dark.

They headed across the empty outdoor exhibit, their feet crunching the snow. They walked along a fake mountainside and arrived at Little Bighorn's cave. One man scanned the zoo grounds, reassuring himself that they hadn't been seen. He was tall and lanky, with a thatch of fire-engine red hair. Charlie Red. With a sweep of his arm, he invited the other man into the cave.

Draped in a black trench coat, the second man wore

a fedora hat with a wide circular brim. As he ducked his head to enter the cave, he uttered a few words to Charlie.

"Nicely done, Mr. Red."

His voice was so gravelly and hoarse that he hardly sounded human. Something seemed wrong with his vocal cords, or his tongue, or his lungs, or all three. He sounded as if his fleshy insides were rotting.

Charlie Red nodded. Then he stood by and watched as the Shadowist disappeared into the cave—the cave with a portal into the Secret Zoo.

Minutes after leaving Rhinorama, Charlie Red opened the door to the main power facility for the Clarksville City Zoo, a small building near the entrance. Once inside, he unclipped his walkie-talkie and raised it to his lips.

"I'm at the front power station. Confirming authorization to restore power."

Mr. Darby's voice came through the speaker. "Charles, we're ready on this end. Please proceed." As Charlie Red used his flashlight to find the proper switches, Mr. Darby added, "Excellent emergency plan, Charles. The prairie dogs, the chickadees—everything worked perfectly. Even Blizzard and Little Bighorn arrived in time. And hiding the zoo in darkness was just outstanding! I think we can be confident that our actions were not spotted by

Outsiders. And we can be certain none of the sasquatches escaped."

Charlie located the switches and turned them on. "Thank you, sir."

"Tank and I are still working with the Constructors. Again, I applaud you. Everything worked according to your plan."

The walkie-talkie went silent, and Charlie replaced it on his hip. He stepped outside and watched the lights blink on across the landscape. Under his breath, he said, "I know, old man. Everything is going *exactly* according to my plan."

With that, Charlie Red closed the door and headed back to his post.

Read on for a preview of the next book in the series,

THE SECRET ZOO

TRAPS AND SPECTERS

❧ CHAPTER 1 ❧

INTO THE SHADOWS

He moved across the Clarksville Zoo. In the midnight sky, clouds slipped across a bright moon, claiming its light. Throughout the zoo, animals slept. Most of them. Others were on patrol. The man lifted his pale face and spotted two koalas clinging to tree branches, their dark, beady eyes turned to him. He saw owls, orangutans, and a red panda chewing on a bamboo leaf. They were watching for the man the Secret Society feared most. The Shadowist. DeGraff.

He sneered. The animals were stupid. All of them.

Toward the middle of the grounds, he stepped into

Flamingo Fountain, a glass building in which a marble fountain sprayed streams of water straight up. The drone and splash of the artificial spring grew louder and louder until it became the only sound. He walked through a cloud of cool mist, squinting. Then he stepped back outside, the door easing shut behind him.

He rolled his shoulders to settle the two heavy packs across his back and rounded Metr-APE-olis. Near Koala Kastle, he spotted a few otters posted in the bushes. Their twitching snouts sniffed the air and traced his passage. He wondered if any of the Descenders could see him. Sam, Solana, Tameron, Hannah—were any of them watching?

The shadowy rooftops of the surrounding neighborhood resembled the peaks of tiny, black pyramids. Smoke streamed from their chimneys, and a few large antennas looked like the cleanly picked bones of strange animals. He spotted a monkey jumping from one house to another. A police-monkey, on patrol. It would spend all night secretly leaping across the rooftops in its tireless circle of the zoo.

The man reached the west entrance, where a bulb buzzed overhead and a cone of light fell across a concrete path that led to a small, wrought-iron gate. He glanced over his shoulders and slipped into a booth beside the path. Inside, a guard sat in a chair, his feet propped up on a small desk. He was gnawing on the end of a toothpick, rolling it across his lips. The two exchanged nods. Then the man carefully set one of his backpacks at the feet of the guard, who quickly looked down at it.

"This it?" the guard asked.

The man nodded.

"When?"

"Soon. In the meantime, just make sure no one finds it."

"You got it, boss."

Their conversation ended, and the guard began again to noisily pick at his teeth. The man stared him up and down and decided he didn't look much different. Not yet.

The man moved to a window and scanned the trees along the perimeter wall. Somewhere in them, animals were posted, hoping to spot the Shadowist advancing on the zoo. In almost a century, it had never happened. And except for the few times Noah and his friends had glimpsed him, he'd never been seen at all.

The man intended to change this. Tonight.

He reached around and patted his remaining backpack, ensuring everything was there. It was. He turned, slipped out of the booth, and quietly stepped through the gate. Now outside the zoo, he sank into the cover of the trees along the concrete wall, dead leaves crinkling beneath his weight. He hunkered in the thick underbrush and eased the backpack off his shoulders.

He waited. He watched the treetops. Nothing stirred. He was certain he hadn't been seen by any of the animals.

A line of bats flew past, but he had no reason to worry about them. They'd see him, but they wouldn't notice him.

He waited a few minutes, then dumped the contents of his pack. Seeing them lying there—realizing what they were—he suddenly became nervous. He glanced all around to reassure himself that he was alone.

On the ground lay a trench coat, gloves, and a hat.

First he gathered up the coat, which was long and leather. He stood, fed his arms through its sleeves, and let its length spill down his legs. Next he donned the gloves, finger by finger. Finally he put on the hat. It was a fedora with a tall crown and a wide brim that bent down over his face.

The man pulled up his collar, tipped the hat down to mask his eyes, then fled, his open trench coat fluttering behind him like a cape. He went swiftly from one point to the next, keeping cover under the trees and in the deeper shadows. They were watching, of this he was certain. From the trees, the rooftops, the sky, the ground—owls and bats and tarsiers.

He dashed across a backyard and hurdled a short fence, his long coat slipping across the sharp pickets. He dodged behind a tree and pressed his back flat against the trunk. He listened for movement in the treetops. Nothing. He pushed off and hurried across the lawn, the edges of his coat snapping. He sank into the shadow of a small shed. From beneath the curved brim of his hat, he turned his eyes to the star-spotted sky. No owls, no bats.

Something moved on a rooftop, two houses down. He peered out and tried to extract shapes from the darkness. Smoke plumed from a chimney, tree branches swayed, billowy clouds drifted across the sky, but nothing else.

Then, suddenly, two silhouettes rose on the rooftop. Two creatures—police-monkeys, no doubt—charged to the edge of the house and lunged six or seven feet to the next one, their dark forms falling into the shadows there.

He slipped inside the shed and eased the door shut, careful not to make a sound. He wrinkled his nose at the stinging smells: fertilizer, paints, and rust. The small space was silent—no wind, no creaking branches, no drone of faraway cars. He leaned toward a small window and peered out. After a few minutes, the monkeys rose and bounded to the next house, disappearing again. Several minutes later, they rose, ran forward, and jumped to the next roof.

He smiled. It was too easy to fool the Secret Society.

Of course it helped that he knew their plan.

He waited a few more minutes, allowing time for the

monkeys to get farther down the neighborhood, then slipped out the door. He headed across the backyard, keeping again to the shadows. He ran between two houses and ducked behind a hedge in a front yard. In all directions, the treetops were perfectly still—he hadn't been seen.

He ran from the bushes and dashed across the street. In the new yard, he set his back against a tree and scanned the treetops again. No movement of any kind.

He turned to the house. Two stories high and made of brick, it stood behind bushes that were groomed into different shapes. A porch lay beneath a wide picture window with closed curtains. He ran across the lawn and jumped onto the stoop. Leaning forward, he peered through a slit between the curtains. The flickering light of a television revealed a girl sitting on a couch, alone.

He smiled a wicked smile. Then he lifted his gloved hand and pecked with a fingertip against the glass.

❧ CHAPTER 2 ❧

OUT OF THE SHADOWS

Ella's eyes jumped from the TV to the front door. Had she heard something? Because her mom was playing cards at Mrs. Carson's, Ella was alone in the house.

The sound came again, a simple *tap*.

She swatted the television remote like a bug and the room fell into darkness. The new silence seemed to have an actual presence—a ghost that had crept into the room.

"Hello?" she asked.

Tap!

She looked out the picture window and realized the curtains weren't completely drawn. Peering through the gap, she saw nothing but a long sliver of the night. Was someone out there? Megan? Perhaps Marlo or another animal from the Secret Zoo?

She bounced off the couch, stepped into the front hall, and yanked the door open. The only thing separating her from the outside was a flimsy screen door. The cold air washed across her body.

"Meg—that you?"

No answer.

She took a deep breath and the cold rushed into her lungs. She cracked open the creaky screen door and peered across the porch. No one.

"Hello? Marlo?"

Wind rustled leaves on the ground.

As she stepped out, the screen door slamming behind her made her jump. The cold of the concrete rose through the rubbery soles of her fluffy pink slippers. The wind collected in the cavity of the porch, whipping her ponytail about. She wrapped her arms over her chest, moved to a place with a good view of her yard, and stared into the darkness.

"Hello?" she asked again.

Nothing. Just leaves tumbling and grass bending under the breath of the sky.

Across the street, a treetop began to shake. Ella peered at it but couldn't see much in its inky web of branches. Then something small shot through the air and disappeared into the tree's silhouette. The limb became still, then the *something small* flew back out and etched a path through the sky in the direction of the Clarksville Zoo.

Ella felt a fresh chill work across her body—a chill that this time hadn't been brought on by the cold. She knew the thing headed toward the zoo was an owl. And she knew what this meant.

As she turned to rush inside, she saw movement out of the corner of her eye, and she stopped. Someone had just stepped out from behind a tall evergreen, a man in a billowy trench coat with the collar turned up. He wore boots and gloves and a hat with a wide, circular brim.

The Shadowist.

After tapping on her window to lead her outside, he'd hidden behind the tree. Now he stood with his back to the street, his arms down, his legs braced far apart, his face masked in the deep shadows of his hat. In the wind, his open coat rolled and snapped.

Ella looked down her neighborhood. How long would it take for the owl to reach the zoo? For the guards and Descenders to arrive? She turned back to DeGraff. Her heart banged against her chest. She couldn't bear the silence any longer.

"What . . . what do you want?"